CAPRI FILE

CAPRI FILE

AMANDA PRANTERA

BLOOMSBURY

First published 2001
This paperback edition published 2002

Copyright © 2001 by Amanda Prantera

The moral right of the author has been asserted

Bloomsbury Publishing Plc, 38 Soho Square, London W1D 3HB

A CIP catalogue record is available from the British Library

ISBN 0 7475 5791 8

Typeset by Hewer Text Ltd, Edinburgh
Printed by Clays Ltd, St Ives plc

To: Pina@her.new.home

'. . . she had
A heart . . . how shall I say? . . . too soon made glad'
                                    – Robert Browning

From: salvia@libero.it
To: sparks@bookhound.com
Subject: to order
Date: Tue, Jan 11, 2000, 10.56 a.m.

Dear Mr/Ms Sparks/Parks or just plain Sparks – I read your ad in the *LRB* and would like you to look out for me, if possible, second-hand copies of the following – condition no object, just as long as they are readable:

Peyrefitte, Roger – *The Exile of Capri* (Panther 1970). Or else, failing that, original French edition, entitled *L'Exilé de Capri* and published don't know when. (Fifties? Sixties?)

Fersen, Jacques – *Et le feu s'éteignit sur la mer . . .* (Paris 1909).

Plus any photograph books showing Capri at the turn of the last century (meaning the twentieth – 1890s to 1920s or thereabouts.)

Thank you for your help. I look forward to hearing from you asap. Yrs sincerely, Lola Salvia d'Acquaviva.

From: salvia@libero.it
To: sparks@bookhound.com
Subject: Capri books
Date: Thu, Jan 13, 2000, 6.24 p.m.

Dear Mr Parks, Thanks for your prompt reply. Yes of course I mean readable in the sense of decipherable, and yes, I know the two novels are going to be difficult to find. I'm *on* Capri at the present – that's where I'm writing from – and in the bookshops here there's not a sign of either, in any language, not even Italian, so I won't grumble even if the search should take you months. (Though I hope it'll turn out to be less, as I need the material desperately for work purposes.) If it's of any help, Fersen's full name was Comte Jacques d'Adelsward Fersen (maybe with an umlaut somewhere, not sure but if you like I can go to the grave-yard to check). The row of other dots after *mer* . . . is part of the title, and you're right, it gave rise to lots of rude comments at the time. Hardly surprising when you consider that Fersen was rich and druggy and reserved to the point of standoffish, and the book was apparently *not* all that brilliant, and Capri's foreign community was a cage of clawing felines. Peyrefitte's novel, *The Exile of Capri*, is in fact based on Fersen's life story, Fersen having been exiled from Capri for ALL ROUND BAD BEHAVIOUR.

Photo book sounds perfect so please send straight off first class. I've an idea you're not meant to e-mail credit card nos. so I'll fax mine to you instead when I go down to the shops, or else ring you direct. Many thanks for your help so far. Yours, Lola (S d'A).

From: salvia@libero.it
To: sparks@bookhound.com
Subject: and object
Date: Fri, Jan 14, 2000, 3.24 p.m.

Dear Simon, nice to talk to you over the phone. Sorry to have disappointed you with the title of my second message. I wrote 'to order' in the first quite by chance, because that was the object of my writing: ordering books. I had no idea that 'Subject' came up on your screen – my headings are all in Italian, and I have: *A, Data, Da*, and *Oggetto* instead, which means object. See? From now on I will try to cater for your low taste in puns.

Thanks for all the trouble you're taking. *Painters on Capri* I have already. Look forward to the arrival of the other volume, though, which judging from the sample photo seems absolutely ideal: artists' studios and aspidistras and naked youths posing for kinky old Krauts – just what I need to spur my flagging imagination. Yrs, Lola.

PS Nothing much here to envy, I assure you. Weather is dreary at present, island is sagging in the millennium aftermath with spent fireworks cartons everywhere, and I'm all alone save for my dog Mitzi and the germ of an idea which will not, *will* not sprout. Some romance, some glamour, I bet you're better off in Ladbroke Grove. L.

From: salvia@libero.it
To: sparks@bookhound.com
Subject: I'm writing about – or trying to
Date: Mon, Jan 17, 2000, 2.45 p.m.

Dear Simon, must disappoint you again but I am not a proper writer. Didn't mean to give the impression I was either. Sorry if I did. The situation is this: I have time on my hands, and am going through a rather tricky phase in my private life, and since I know quite a bit about Capri from having spent the last seven summers here, not to mention countless weekends, I thought it might be a good idea to settle myself in for the winter and write something connected with the island, though I still don't quite know what. Friends suggested a history, but I've discovered I'm too ignorant; my mum said a cook book, but I'm a lousy cook. (I will spare you what my husband said: he's bent on sabotage anyway, and we've just spent the whole weekend quarrelling on this account.) My own idea – after several attempts at the literary high ground and sobering chutes to the base – is more a thriller or a detective story, set at the turn of the twentieth century. Hence the books and hence the research. Capri is full of mysteries and soggy little corners where the sun doesn't reach. Don't know if you've ever been here, or if so what impression it made on you, but

7

I remember on my own first visit being struck by the fact that everything I saw – every beautiful magical thing – had an underbelly to it that wasn't beautiful at all. The smell of sea and herbs, for example, that wafted all over the place and that I would draw into my lungs, intoxicated, only to be brought up short by an intrusive whiff of pee or the carcass of a dead cat. Or the room I slept in, with its terracotta tiles and sunlit terrace, and a cascade of plumbago all around it, framing the marina, blue against blue to take your breath away, and peaches on the table, and a fragrant linen-clad bed, and then – horrorbins – a gruesome patch of damp in the corner, where the air-conditioner had leaked and bled into the rock, breeding mushrooms. This chiaroscuro contrast is what set me going in the first place, and what makes me think the island, for all its tourist image of sun and wine and tarantella, would make a good backdrop for a pretty sombre tale, if only I could tell it. Heart of Darkness. Rotten core. Gilded tombs that do worms enfold – that sort of lark.

It's also what led me to Fersen. As I say, there are dozens of scandals to choose from – the arms manufacturer Krupp who committed suicide after doing a total Herr Ventvorth Brüster and tottering down the hill to live it up in a grotto with his band of new-found *Freundlings*; the painter Allers who fled the island overnight to escape a pederasty charge; the girl who killed herself for love of the writer Malaparte, and plenty more besides – but *listen* to this description from a visitor to Fersen's home, the Villa Lysis, about sixty years after it had lain empty, following his death:

At the end of the path we found the villa. It was dark and deserted, overgrown by creepers and shadowed by cypress trees. Over the doorway was the inscription: AMORI ED DOLORI SACRUM. Mananà turned the key in the lock, and we crossed the floor on tiptoe. From the dusty chandeliers an ancient smell of incense wafted down. On the floor moth-eaten cushions were still strewn, ivory trays were still lying on the ebony tables. On the walls hung classical nudes in the style of Alma-Tadema. Beneath the smell of stale incense and musty cushions, I thought I could just sense a vague whiff of opium . . .

See what I mean? Stuff this in your jasper opium pipe – *if* you have time, and compassion for my writer's block – and come back to me with criticisms and/or suggestions. They would come like manna to the starving. Yrs, Lola.

See my brain, how trite its workings? I write Mananà, and straightaway out comes manna – a word I haven't used since schooldays, if then. Ah well: probably better that than pussyfooting around trying to be original.

From: salvia@libero.it
To: sparks@bookhound.com
Subject: to terrible bouts of logorrhoea
Date: Wed, Jan 19, 2000, 5.14 p.m.

Simon – No, I beg of you, **NOT** Tiberius. Classical-based mystery stories are so *nerdy*. OK, he might easily have been the victim of a smear-campaign, and all the talk about torture and whim killings and the underwater fellatio with the shoal of little *pisciculi* swimming about underneath him nibbling at his genitals (how did they *breathe*, poor little beggars?) might easily have been false, but so what? Quite honestly who gives a *ficus* any more? Now we have the Oval Room the goings-on in the Blue Grotto of two thousand years ago leave everyone cold. Or not?

Are *you* a nerd? I didn't ask. But if you are, rest assured that our correspondence keeps me so happy that I wouldn't mind a bit. I'm slightly inclined that way myself.

You ask about me. Well, I haven't got a scanner or all that posh equipment you've got so I can't send you a picture straight off, but I'm roughly as follows: thirty-seven, small-ish, thinnish, darkish, with very short hair and rather a wide mouth that I used to hate, before having ruefully to acknowledge it was in fact my best feature. Eyes: slanted-cum-slitty, nose short, ears large. A pixie face, I suppose, is what it is, much as I revile pixies. Two and a half years ago I had to have my ovaries removed as a result of a burst cyst, and this has not added exactly to my femininity, never very rampant in the first place, but *me la cavo*, as the Italian saying goes: I pass muster, I get by.

Mitzi is an Alsatian, eight, also spayed, but in her case the op has done wonders for her female attributes, tits in particular. V unfair.

You, on the other hand, could send me a photo. (Unless you are *monstrous*: in which case take a leaf from my book and hide behind a verbal description. In reality I am seventy-three, large, white and bloated, with long grey witchy tresses and a mouth like a shrivelled prune . . .

No, no, relax, the first description is closer to the mark. But there again, look into yourself and ask, Would it matter? We hit it off all right in this dimension, no? Why bother about adding a third?

Now to the defence of my plan. Does it have to be Fersen, you ask? Well, I think it does and for various reasons. The first – the clash between showy exterior and putrid core – I've already explained, and Fersen embodies it like no one else who's ever lived here. (And there have been plenty of other candidates. Capri attracts poseurs like a magnet: if you want a list I'll draw one up for you). Poor Comte Jacques, I have nothing against him – in fact he seems to have been rather shy and kind and nicely mannered compared to the other residents of the period – but his whole life, like Ludwig of Bavaria's (ever seen that indoor lake at Neuschwanstein or wherever? God, that grotto's grotty), was spent fussing over a kind of elaborate cardboard construction, designed to screen the harshness of reality and replace it with a simulacrum of perfect beauty. Result, like Ludwig's: shoddiness of tragic proportions.

That's point one. Point two – closely connected to point one – is that Fersen was a boy fancier, and the more I think of it the more I become convinced that a paedo-story would be just the thing for me to work on. Capri in that period was a Mecca for homosex tourism, and besides, it's a perversion that fascinates me, don't know why – just can't get my mind round it. (Serial killer possibly even better, but the island is too small to contain a criminal of such proportions. If there was one he would have to emigrate: you can hardly sneeze here without everyone knowing it, let alone butcher a string of non-consenting people.)

Point three is that Villa Fersen, or Villa Lysis as its proper name is, is practically on my doorstep and has had a kind of hold on me ever since I first set foot on the island, and I WANT TO WRITE ABOUT IT. Definitely more than Tiberius anyway, whose villa is also in my backyard, so to speak.

Is that enough to win you over? Will you help me (changing the names and everything) invent a paedo-plot, set in this setting, at the time I have chosen? Or will you dodge and come up with another nerd's delight? Or will you cry off, horrified by this deluge of gabble from – Mad Lola of Capri.

PS No sign of my book. Perhaps a courier would be best for the others – if they ever come in. Money's one problem I don't have, and for that I thank my clever dead dad and count myself very lucky.

*　　*　　*

PPS Would you be an angel and look out for me a standard textbook on – yes, you've guessed it – paedophilia, what else.

From: salvia@libero.it
To: sparks@bookhound.com
Subject: still vague, but becoming clearer
Date: Thu, Jan 20, 2000, 10.35 p.m.

You want the Capri pseuds? You actually *want* them? Well, you've asked for them so here they are:

Turn to p. 41 of the book you wanted to send me about the painters, and top left you will see two rather sweet old fogeys poring over a book together. Flemish interior, phials and potions as befits an Alchemist's workshop, and in the foreground the sitters themselves with their beards and robes and velvet rasta berets and earflaps *à la* Thomas More. They are the middle-of-the-heap American painters, *Elihu Vedder* and *Charles Caryl Coleman*, posing as Rembrandts. In another shot they pose as Michelangelos. They look dead serious in both guises: my guess is that they either had a malicious stylist or else they saw themselves as geniuses. Possibly both.

Underneath, same page, roughly same date, 1920, observe the illustrated birthday verses penned to Coleman by his much younger muse-cum-mistress, *Rose O'Neil*. Painter she may have been but she was no draughtswoman. And no poet either:

Once more to garland him, the Graceful
 With that great Don. (Who on earth was Don?
Giovanni?)
 He. (scrawl: I think it's meant to represent a *Sphinx*
but it looks like a ruddy *Afghan hound*) *of the Wind-
mills*
 And the noblest eyes,
 Who saved the slipping vesture of Romance . . .

Get a load of that R in Romance, its legs almost reach the
bottom of the page – can't coax my computer to do anything like it. And what about the slipping vesture? Isn't it
scrummy?

And talk about slipping, we could *glisser* ourselves – to
another phoney who knocks this trio practically out of the
arena: the Marchesa Casati. Dyed her dogs mulberry and
mauve to match her Fortuny clothes; doped herself up to her
kohl-rimmed eyeballs; traipsed around with gazelles on
leashes, attended by a black bodyguard dusted all over with
gold-leaf. Terrific stuff. I have a piccy of her here in another
book, practically garrotted by beads, staring out mournfully
into the lens, with an autograph note underneath dated
1913: *The flesh is nought but a spirit pledged to Death*.

Sorry. Long interruption here. Friend came round, neigh-
bour name of Nico – would-be writer like me, and like me
in a terrible sentimental imbroglio – and we've been making
a taco supper to try and cheer each other up. Whatever I
was droning on about earlier has gone right out of my head.

Re-reading what I've written, though, I've come to the
conclusion that the period I fancy is definitely the right one:
some of these oddballs are too good to throw away; they
just cry out for recycling as minor characters in the plot. In

particular my heart is set on using the Misses Woolcott-Perry, Kate and Saidee, but I'm too tired to describe them to you now. '*Thespians* in aspect, dear, *thespians*.' Tomorrow I'm going to walk Mitzi down to the Villa Fersen – all posh and restored now, maybe someone's bought it, it was up for sale only a few months ago – and see if I can find a caretaker or someone who'll let me in to have a look round. Gardens at least, if not inside. Then I'll let you know my impressions. All the best and hope it's not the dreaded flu – Lola.

PS Don't see why you apologise about the photo. You look sweet in it – much more handsome than I imagined. Intellectuals *shouldn't* be too good-looking, you know, a) it would be unfair and b) it would make them too obvious and detract from their aura. This rule in my book applies to both sexes, and you *almost* break it.

From: salvia@libero.it
To: sparks@bookhound.com
Subject: title invented in a hurry
Date: Fri, Jan 21, 2000, 2.39 p.m.

Photo book arrived. Perfect. Many, *many* thanks. Message about Russians arrived too. Things are a bit awkward at the moment and I shan't be able to answer till Sunday night or Monday. Haven't even got time to think up a decent subject title, so have just put that, as it was the first and feeblest that came into my head. Never mind, eh. All the best, Lola.

From: salvia@libero.it
To: sparks@bookhound.com
Subject: s of the Tsar
Date: Tue, Jan 25, 2000, 4.17 p.m.

Si. Hi. Sorry I didn't reply yesterday either, I just wasn't in the mood. Boring things, won't burden you with them.

Or, no, perhaps I will. Have you ever been through a major crisis with a partner? Do tell me – if telling a relative stranger like me doesn't bug you. My only really serious relationship to date is this seven-year stint with Ferdinando, and I'm totally at a loss as to what's going on. Comparing notes might help.

Nico does what he can, poor sweet – acts as punchball and dustbin and shoulder to cry on – but being gay, his notes don't quite tally with mine. Capri's a bit empty in the winter and apart from him and the cleaning lady who pops in twice a week to tidy up there's no one much to talk to. I suppose you guessed that already from all this babble.

Sudden thought: perhaps you're gay too? Are you, Simone? No matter, straight or gay, more info on any aspect of the matter would be appreciated. And now to work, which is my own way out of the slough. The Russians, you say: political intrigue and Lenin and Gorky and company. Ummm. Yes. Well. Probably brilliant idea in the hands of someone else, but I doubt it would be in mine. The faces on the photo you marked for me are much too *morally charged* somehow, and I am much too frivolous to handle such a group or such a theme. Politics is Sanskrit to me. All those worthy woolly cardigans: a close-knit batch of exiles in every sense. And that reproduction of the Mona Lisa in the background . . . Mona Lisa, of all things, that's as close to Italy as these people ever got: a token print of the Mona Lisa propped on their bookcase. Capri was nothing to them, just a convenient perching place on their migratory path. There they sit, physically on Italian soil, while you can see that each and every one of them is Versts away inside their heads. No, sorry to be such a Molotov (or whichever it was who was always turning down proposals) but I'm much more at home with the lightweights and a bourgeois individualist theme like murder.

Although if it's *mass* murder we're talking about, then Lenin . . . Oho, something tells me I'd better not go any further in this direction if we're to remain friends. Are you a red, Si? Not that it'd matter to me if you were, but I think you might take objection to *my* colour, which is so mixed-up and cloudy it's like the liquid painters keep their brushes in. Only black is missing. Can you go on corresponding with such a motley creature? I do hope so.

Anyway, to return to the book, it's too late now for Romans or Russians or anybody because I have a NEW IDEA which I am TOTALLY SOLD ON, and that is: a kind of Capri Witch Project, with a group of Californian hippies or flower people or whatever they called themselves, camping out in Villa Fersen in the seventies – eighties, when it had reached the nadir of its decline, and investigating some past mystery which took place there but still has ramifica-

22

tions that extend into the present, and treading on people's toes they shouldn't, and dropping off their perches one by one. Ten Little Californians, sort of thing. And then there were ZEEERO. What about that?

Haven't let on about this to my husband Ferdinando yet, or I would get a broadside of scorn (everything I do nowadays seems to earn me that). But you should *see* the villa, Simon, really you should. At least, you should see it as it was then, in the time I want to write about, before the restoration squad got busy. It makes THE PERFECT SETTING for a thriller. Even now that end of the island is a bit creepy; even Mitzi thinks so: her fur went all spiky along her back when we went that way on our walk. And that's not all: I couldn't get anything out of the caretaker, who just barked at me over the intercom to go away, but there was an old geezer I met on the way back who told me there's been a fairly recent tragedy linked to the villa too. Well, not really linked, but during the renovation work a couple of winters back there was apparently a boy – a little local boy – who fell to his death off the cliffs nearby. Wonder why I never heard of this. Ferdinando must have known: our villa here was being done up too at roughly the same time, and he was back and forth constantly that year, overseeing the work. Suppose he didn't want to upset me.

So. Add this death to that of a bricklayer killed during the building of the original house in 1905 or thereabouts; that of Fersen's housekeeper in 1913, who slipped on the rocks in a drunken stupor and did a bungee jump minus bungee; and that of Fersen himself ten years later, in a thunderstorm, in the middle of the night, from an overdose of opium, with his friends bustling round afterwards trying to prettify the corpse with rouge and rosebuds, and you have quite a basketful of disasters to choose from, don't you think?

Another idea. What about bringing in a bit of borderline supernatural? Killer in the present and Ghosts from the past as well. Like that I could still make use of the *fin de siècle* atmosphere and bring in all the oddballs, Casatis and Woolcott-Perrys and Co, and my research wouldn't go wasted. One of the hippies could claim to be psychic and have visions and things, which on one level you could treat as real and on another as a by-product of hysteria. Get your teeth into that one. Or into me, if you prefer: I certainly deserve it for changing my mind so often – Lola.

PS The Freud sounds a bit daunting, I was thinking of something more bite-size, but anyway please send. (Teeth – bite – honestly, must do something about my style!)

From: salvia@libero.it
To: sparks@bookhound.com
Subject: of dispute in a graveyard
Date: Thu, Jan 27, 2000, 3.16 p.m.

Simon, goodness you must be a nice person. Yesterday evening, when nothing had come through from you, I thought, that's it, I've really pissed him off now, and I can't really blame him because it's my own stupid fault – turning down all his suggestions, and asking all those rude questions about his private life and droning on boringly about mine, which is even worse. And now here comes this lovely long letter that has *made* my day, no exaggeration. (Otherwise rather empty, as it's freezing here at the moment and I could only lure Mitzi out mid-morning when the sun had got going, and not for very long at that. More about where we went in a second.)

Straight, eh? Well, I thought so somehow. Wasn't *that* far out over the politics either, was I? Only for some reason I'd figured you out as more committed. Glad you're not; glad you're a dreamer instead of a marcher. Seven serious partners, on the other hand, came as a bit of a surprise. Quite honestly, unless you're lying about your age, I don't see how you could have had the time. Who gave who the push in cases 2, 4, 5 and 6? You don't say. And is no. 7 still going strong, or is the one you're with now no. 8, and if so, why isn't she on the list? You don't make that quite clear either. Most helpful to me was the Rebecca story, no. 3, because of that kind of limbo period you lived through together towards the end, when the barrier that had grown up between you had turned into such a prickly hedge that neither of you liked to touch it. You explain that beautifully: that impasse, stalemate or whatever it was in which you found yourselves locked. (Stale Mate – that sounds familiar OK). You say you recommend storm tactics – grip the hedge by the thorns. If I can summon up courage – because I'm a terrible coward where scenes are concerned – I will try these over the weekend.

God, it nearly *is* the weekend. Well, perhaps next weekend . . .

Let's talk of something else. Ah yes, my walk. Guess where I took Mitzi? Up to the cemetery, just for a bit of jollity for a change. (No, in fact I went there because I wanted to check out the tomb of the boy who was killed near Villa Fersen, whose name, I've since discovered, was Antonio Vito, or Tonino for short.) And guess what happened there? I found the grave quite easily, in the larger, Catholic part of the cemetery, and I read the inscription and took a look at the photograph – *dear* little face, rather like the Pakistani kid in *East is East*; did you see that? Impish mouth, mournful eyes – really tears at your heart to find an image like that on a gravestone. And then, on impulse, or maybe because it struck me sort of subliminally or whatever that it was about the only grave lacking in flowers (which in Italy is strange: the non-Catholic part of the cemetery is admittedly pretty bare – save for Gracie Fields – but the main section is blooming all over like a Dutch bulb field), I

26

went to the bin where all the trimmings and leftovers are dumped and retrieved a little pot of heather someone had discarded, and broke off some twigs and twisted them into a little plait, and then I laid it on the shelf in front of the stone. And as I did so, a woman who'd been tending several other graves round about – one of these cemetery buffs you get in this country, who spend hours fussing over other people's plots as well as their own – surged forward and knocked the heather off again.

Didn't take it off; knocked it off. I must have looked astounded. I was astounded. 'Nothing to do with him, poor little *piccirillo*,' she said before I could utter a sound. 'It's them, the family. *Fetentielli*. Nasty lot. They deserve no favours, and when it's up to me, I see to it they get none.' Then she looked a bit taken aback herself, as if in her haste she might have done something she'd regret, and asked me a bit quakily if by chance I was a relative.

I said no, and she looked dead relieved. But only for a moment, because no sooner had she got her bounce back than she got all bossy and suspicious again and wanted to know who I was if I wasn't family, and whereabouts in the graveyard were *my* deceased relations if I had any, and what was I doing there if I hadn't; and instead of asking questions, the way I'd planned, I found myself answering them. Fatal, because once she'd placed me as the *inglese* from Villa Acquaviva, that was that. The Capresi will gossip with Capresi and they'll gossip with total outsiders, but they won't gossip with insiders who aren't Capresi, which is what I suppose I am. A hybrid, a half-and-halfer. Ferdinando's family have owned land and property here since 1850 or thereabouts, but they've never lived here, never really belonged. In fact, as his old mum remarked in shrivelling disapproval when she handed me the keys of the villa, I'm probably the very first member to actually spend an entire winter here. Christmas and New Year is OK, but the rest of the winter – dreadfully *cafone*.

Anyway, as I was leaving, I bent to unhook Mitzi's lead from the gate where I'd tied her, and out of the corner of my eye I saw the woman grind my little posy of heather in the dust with her heel and then spit on it. Charming. But in fact I think it was less to do with me than with my ma-in-law, who is much better known locally, and *not at all* beloved. People don't notice me enough to slight me, I'm far too inoffensive. Sometimes I even get the impression they're rather sorry for me – being alone so much, I suppose, and my roots in another country.

Must stop now and tackle the fearful hurdle of the first chapter. I think you're right about having a group of English campers, not Americans. Only trouble is I've lived abroad so long I don't think I could quite handle punks like you suggest: their idiom would be just as foreign. Therefore – don't groan, but I've decided to make them a bit Sloaney or maybe I mean preppy. Posse of Oxbridge undergrads on hols – names like Tristram and Olivia. Toffee-nosers. My sort of acquaintances alas, once upon a time. Better to be on home ground, no? Then if it was ever made into a film Hugh Grant could take the lead, unless he was too long in the tooth.

Send you my efforts as soon as I've got anything to show. Keep writing if you can. An e-mail from you would tide me over the weekend – tomorrow is Friday and I've come to dread Fridays a bit. Love, Lola.

From: salvia@libero.it
To: sparks@bookhound.com
Subject: ed to pressure but holding out
Date: Thu, Feb 3, 2000, 5.54 p.m.

Simon, I'm so sorry about this long silence, but I couldn't find the copy of the *LRB* with your number in it, and like a fool I'd forgotten to write it down, or else I'd have called. Please e-mail it to me straightaway and I will write it somewhere safe in letters of bilberry juice – the most indelible liquid I know.

What happened is this. There was a bit of a fracas over the weekend with Ferdinando (don't want to bother you with the details, it wasn't anything out of the ordinary, just the usual Torquemada Twostep: him wanting me back in Naples, me wanting to stay on here, etc., etc.). And during one particularly . . . don't know what to call it quite, let's say animated moment of the discussion my neck got caught in the lead of the computer and down it went on to the floor with a crash.

No serious damage, thank God. No brain trauma, no irreversible coma or anything like that, only a touch of amnesia and a bruised mouse, but it's taken till today for the technician to come round and sort things out. Because here we are not on the mainland and we dance to an island tempo all our own.

In the meantime I have not been sitting around on my fanny. I haven't tackled the novel of course because I've pretty well lost the knack of writing with a pen, but I've been sleuthing around on the tracks of poor little dead Tonino, and, SIMON, don't think I'm just inventing dramas for a bit of distraction, although that's always a possibility, but I've come to the conclusion that there is something not quite straightforward about the circumstances of his death. Maybe even something MYSTER-IOUS. It's very weird. People are so cagy about it. So far, counting the lady in the cemetery, I've spoken to four different people, asking them what they remember, and here, pretty well verbatim, are the reactions I got:

Assunta the cleaning lady (with a definite little start of surprise, immediately suppressed): Tonino Vito? Yes, I think I remember Tonino Vito. So many Vitos; breed like rabbits. He used to work on the ferry service. Smarmy fellow – think he moved to Ischia.

Me: No, Assunta. This one was a little boy, who died. About two years ago. Not far from here, on the rocks above Villa Fersen. He had an accident and fell.

Assunta: Did he? Well. Children. Nasty place.

Me: Don't you remember him at all? Don't you remember anything about it?

Assunta: Why should I?

Me: I don't know. It's not every day a thing like that happens. So close to here and everything. I thought you might . . .

Assunta: Did you know about it, *Duchessa*?

Me: Silence. (She calls me Lola as a rule and the title came like a slap. I should have simply countered that it happened in winter when I wasn't here, but didn't think of this till it was too late.)

Assunta (much more dextrous. You can see she is glad to be shot of the subject, though, by the way she spins round and scurries back into the kitchen, throwing the remark over her shoulder and leaving it there): Well, nor did I.

Carmine, my ma-in-law's handyman and part-time gardener: Vito? Vito? A boy, you say? Fell off a cliff, did he? Hrrach. (Gob of spit into the iris patch.) Most likely nosing round in things that didn't concern him.

No comeback from me, as the way this is uttered discourages any further talk.

Signora Luotto, cashier lady at grocer's and generally quite pally (not that much older than me, probably, in calendar terms, but so much larger and different that I think I must stir up her protective instincts. She's always pinching at my arm and sighing and trying to sell me fattening things like chitterlings and chocolate): Ah, that story. Well, it was some years back now, wasn't it. I can't say I remember much about it. We've got some nice fresh *tagliolini, Signora bella*, if you'd like some.

Me: Two. It was two years ago.

Signora Luotto: Was it now? Fancy. No *tagliolini*? Then that'll be four thousand lire. Fifteen with yesterday.

Me: Do you know the family at all?

Signora Luotto: (Tart cluck of denial).

Me: It must have been terrible for them, losing a son like that.

Signora Luotto: Snort of I don't know what.

But whatever it is, it seems to be directed at me as well,

so I belt up. (One serious flaw, if I want to pursue this matter, is that I am not leathery enough to make a good detective: it's no good minding people's reactions, you just have to forge ahead.)

And that's all, you will say? That's all the evidence you have to build a mystery on? Yes, that's all, and written down like that I agree it looks slender. But, Simon, it was the *way* they all spoke, and the way they *looked* at me as they spoke. I can't explain: disapproving, disconcerted: as if I was being tactless in bringing up the subject. No, there's definitely something fishy there. What would you do next, if you were me? Who would you turn to to find out more?

Don't worry, if you're going rock climbing I shan't expect your answer till Monday or Tuesday of next week. Have fun. I've got a nice weekend ahead too. Ferdinando flies to New York for an auction, and I've got a sweet fat girlfriend coming over from England who he hates, and I love. Careful with those pitons or whatever they're called: it's not only kids can fall. Lola.

From: salvia@libero.it
To: sparks@bookhound.com
Subject: all corny songs turn on – lerve, lerve, lerve
Date: Tue, Feb 8, 2000, 2.32 p.m.

You know, Simon, I really enjoy opening my e-post now. It gives me that feeling I used to get as a child when I stayed with my grandmother and went egg-collecting in her hen house: will there be one in this box? How big? Will it still be warm? Super letter today. Ostrich size at least. So long that I've had to print it out and make notes of the bits that need answering. I'll take them one by one.

1) I can't send you my first chapter: a) because I've nowhere *like* finished it yet, b) because it's on a file and I can't seem to master the procedure for e-mailing files (poor computer of mine, it must be miserable in my hands – when it's not at my feet, being kicked around like a football). And c) because I'm not sure I ever will finish it now, seeing that today Ferdinando sent me an article from the newspaper, the *Repubblica*, about some English novelist who has written a thriller set in Capri at the turn of the last century, which has just been translated into Italian. Can you imagine anything more deflating? A thriller, a mystery

story, 1910 or thereabouts: the reviewer said it was wonderful and captured the atmosphere of place and period so beautifully bla bla bla . . . I could have wept. Ah, well, there's still the cook book, I suppose, still some demand for recipes for almond cake and *limoncello*.

2) Yes, whadderyerknow, I am a duchess. Sort of. In actual fact titles have been legally abolished in Italy for decades, but for some reason or other (it wouldn't be snobbery, now, would it?) they seem to hang around still. A bit like when you spill a box of confetti: you try to clean up, but years later you're still finding the stuff in the floorboards. Make no mistake, though: a southern Italian duchess, or at any rate one like me, must in no way be confused with an English duchess, or even a French one or a German one or a Spanish one (and the list could continue through most of Europe). Grandeur exists in Ferdinando's family, true, but practically all of it is inside the head of his mother, ten per cent in the memory department, ninety in the imagination. Take this for an example: my mum came over to visit just before we got married and a cocktail party was given in her honour at the Palazzo Acquaviva (that part of it that was not occupied by the Bank that rents it). Guess what Ferdinando's mother did. She came to the door to welcome her, grabbed her by the hand, dragged her through the hall without allowing her time to pause and admire so much as a picture or a statue or say hello to a fellow guest – No, no, no. Letter, letter. Com, com. Luke, luke. Lugged her up the stairs to the

first floor and waltzed her at the same pace through room after room of the *piano nobile*, then up another floor to the bedrooms, then up again to what were once the servants' quarters, then up a fourth staircase to the attic, where she chivvied her up a rung ladder and on to the roof and finally brought her to a stop in front of the prized store of water tanks and said, See? See now, your dotter, who she is merrying? Imagine the Duchess of Devonshire doing that at Chatsworth. My mum was totally fazed. No, the Acquavivas are quite a ropy lot really: Ferdinando has an uncle who lives in borderline squalor and has *never left his bed*, that anyone can remember, though perfectly hale in body. He lives with a cinema usherette, who dotes on him, and he spends all his time devising systems for playing the lottery. Matilde, my ma-in-law, passes him off as a failed genius. Perhaps he is. And perhaps he'll make a killing one day. Which would be splendid, as upkeep of the family falls quite heavily on Ferdinando's shoulders as things stand (or fall, in the case of the houses), and indirectly on mine. And this brings me to point

3) You ask about Ferdinando. Who he is. Why I married him. Whether I loved him, whether I still do. Oh Simon, I wish I knew the answers, especially to the first and last. Let me begin with a physical description. Who knows, perhaps enlightenment will filter through to me as I write. Well, he's a good deal older than me, for a start. Eleven years. Making him nearly forty-eight, but he looks much younger – very dark, very thin, very athletic, hardly grey at all. Heightwise

we're not very well matched, because he is over six foot and in restaurants and places I am often taken for his daughter: the other day a waiter asked him if the *piccirilla* (meaning me) would have the same as her *papà*, and he was furious with the man, called him an idiot to his face. If the poor waiter had looked closer, though, he would have realised his mistake: I am no beauty, and Ferdinando is.

(Blast. I keep getting a wide margin here. Why is that? Why won't this para stay in line?) By trade he is an antique dealer – chiefly pictures. He has a degree in economics but has never used it: to keep him at university his ma started selling off bits of family furniture and stuff, and he started helping her out, and the thing sort of took off from there. Or so I've pieced together: he doesn't talk much to me about his past; it's a bit as if, when he married me, he began a new chapter and is loath to go back and re-read. He loves art and beautiful things, paints a bit himself in his spare time, and does a lot of research on history of art, and a friend of his told me recently that he is coming to be recognised as quite an expert on Neapolitan Baroque. (Not a style I'm dotty about. And you?)

Will that do as a sketch? It's only thumbnail, I realise, but implicitly it answers your second question as well: I married him because I was swept off my prosaic little Kensingtony feet by him, and because I was flattered anyone of his glamour could possibly have time for me. And a bit also, probably, because my dad died when I was ten and I was looking for a father figure to replace him; and because my mum was captivated too – by Ferdinando's manners (which can be exquisite when he feels like it and lousy when he doesn't); and because in the setting of Edwardes Square he shone like a bulb in a biscuit tin. If I loved him then??? Can't answer that one. Came to love him? Yes I did, although not in the same way I loved him (*if* I loved him) at the outset: he seemed to have a terrific need of me, much stronger than mine of him, and it was that that bound me to him in the end. Funny, no?

Whether I still love him? Ah, well, seeing that this need of his seems to have abated, I think the present position is this: that I'm in the process of trying not to love him, and sometimes succeeding and sometimes not.

Voilà. Sorry to have turned so telegraphic *en route*, but I discovered that I'm a bit ashamed to talk to you about these things. I must try for more candour. You came clean about being ditched all those times, I don't see why I shouldn't do the same, only just at the moment I'd prefer to chicken out and warp to point . . .

4) Oh, God, this is trickier still. Let me just reassure you that the fall was not entirely but *almost* entirely my own silly fault. I was a dyspraxic child and am therefore a pretty dyspraxic adult as well. Don't please worry on this score: there is violence, but it's not usually of this kind. Now, quick, let me pass to

5) (Sod these silly margins, wish I'd never started fiddling with them.) Haven't found out yet what a Coroner's Report would correspond to in Italy or how to set about gaining access to one, but your idea of consulting the teacher was INSPIRED. Written so much that I'll save up for tomorrow all the things I've

found out. My friend Althea leaves at lunchtime, so I'll have all the afternoon free.

6) Yes, the Freud has arrived OK but I'm not making much headway with him. Bit sticky as I feared. (Oh sod again. Look at that.)

7) Re your last question, I honestly don't know. I've never seen anyone doing it here, but maybe that's because most of the tourists are too old. On Ischia, certainly, they whizz up and down like spiders. Now I must go and make spaghetti. Love and *baci*, Lola.

From: salvia@libero.it
To: sparks@bookhound.com
Subject: continued from yesterday
Date: Thu, Feb 10, 2000, 3.17 p.m.

Come stai, Simone? My darling podgy Althea has left and the weekend looms. But no use getting paranoid: perhaps he won't come, And if he does, perhaps he'll be jet-lagged and sleep all the time. Keep your fingers crossed for me, even if it hinders your typing.

Now to the news I promised. Nothing definite, but a few more little chips to add to the mosaic and amplify the pattern. On Saturday Nico and Althea and I went to the school Tonino used to attend. We spoke – at least Nico did – to some of the children on their way out, trying to see if we could find any ex-classmates. (I knew this was not a good idea, but I couldn't really say so to Nico, who is one of those gays who pride themselves on appearing to be plumb straight, while of course he isn't and doesn't.) Reactions were mostly what you'd expect: giggles, headshakes – the typical *camorra* tilt of the chin in the air, *Moh, Che volite, Nun saccio*. One of the older kids, a bit more hard-boiled, shouted out, *E muorto, no?* He's dead. And laughed like a jackal.

Then, just as I'd warned Nico would happen, out came a

teacher, quivering with righteous anxiety, to suss us out and shoo us away. I did the talking this time. I introduced myself as Althea's interpreter, and said she was a journalist, writing an article for a children's magazine in England about the hazards of rock climbing, and was investigating the accident in which one of the pupils of this school had lost his life. (Cunning, no?) Could she help us?

A bit mollified, she led us into the school and went to call the headmistress, who she said would know more about the matter than she did. Personally she couldn't remember any child dying in a climbing accident, but then she was a newcomer, she'd been transferred from Procida only a year ago.

Procida is – what? – twenty minutes away by boat, if that. I mentioned Tonino's name, but all she did was shake her head and bolt.

The headmistress took some time coming. While we were waiting, Nico stuck his head out of the window and began chatting up the *bidella*, who is – what would she be called in English? Sort of halfway between a cleaner and a matron, only closer to a cleaner. This was a master stroke of genius. From the headmistress, when at last she arrived, we learnt nothing, but *nothing*. Antonio Vito had, yes, been a pupil in this school, and yes, he had been killed in a tragic accident two years previously, but there was nothing in the manner of his death that could possibly interest the readers of Althea's magazine. How did she know that? How could she say it with such certainty? Indignation: how could *we* presume to question her judgement in the matter? None of the children on Capri went in for rock climbing, and it would be nonsense to suggest it. Harmful nonsense. They had their football and their swimming. The only climbing they did was on the frame in the gym, and it had best remain that way. There were hazards enough as it was, what with motorbikes and discothèques and (withering gaze at all three of us) unreliable foreigners. So now, if we would excuse her . . .

I didn't want to excuse her yet in the least, but I could see Nico was keen to be off, so that he could carry on his confab outside with his new lady friend. This he proceeded to do alone – better psychology, we thought – and came galloping after us, crowing victory, about ten minutes later, having obtained the following, quite valuable, snippets of information:

The whereabouts of Tonino's parents' house for a start, plus further confirmation that they are not very highly thought of on the island, and a warning to stay clear of them. People blamed them, according to the *bidella*, for the death of their son, if not materially then morally. He was left too much to his own devices – often skipped school, often came, *when* he came, without proper books or proper elevenses. It wasn't that they grudged him money – sometimes he seemed to have almost too much of that; it was the time, the attention that was lacking. His regular teachers had written him off as just one of those under-achievers who'll leave early and apprentice themselves to a mechanic, all being well, but she'd always had a soft spot for him herself – it must have been those Bambi eyelashes. And apropos of teachers, she also gave Nico the name of a young stop-gap teacher from Naples who'd replaced one of the regulars for several months, round about the time of Tonino's death, and who she said had been fond of him and had taken more trouble with him than most. She said she was pleased people like us were asking after him, never mind if so late in the day, because he'd gone out puff! like a little candle, and nobody had seemed to want to hear or say anything about him, and to her way of thinking it was a sin on all their consciences.

SO YOU SEE. There *is* something odd about the whole thing, and I'm not wasting my time on it, because whatever I discover, even if it's an empty box with no gilt and no worms, I can always use the *idea* for a book afterwards and add cans full of both on my own account. And don't laugh: I really mean to write one in the end, you know. And don't grumble about my inconstancy either: I'll still buy the books I ordered from you if and when they crop up – no matter that I no longer need them, no matter that they're first editions and cost a bomb: I never go back on my word once given. Probably flog them here for double anyway. Much love, L.

From: salvia@libero.it
To: sparks@bookhound.com
Subject: to weekend nerves
Date: Fri, Feb 11, 2000, 4.53 p.m.

Just a quick signal: a wave of my hat on a stick to show I'm here and have received your oh so probing and near-the-knuckle message. I'll answer it Monday, when Ferdinando has left. I'll come clean, I promise: I've never told anyone, it's so shaming, but to you, my far-off e-pen-pal, I think I can tell all, or nearly. You're right, I must tell someone or go crazy.

Where are you off to? Tunbridge Wells? Doesn't sound very mountainous to me.

No, I never call him Ferdie and nor does anyone else. Matilde – his old witch of a mother – calls him Dodo sometimes, but only when she is in a serene mood which is almost never.

Take care (and I mean it seriously, not as a throw-away salute the way most people use it), L.

From: salvia@libero.it
To: sparks@bookhound.com
Subject: ive moan
Date: Mon, Feb 14, 2000, 2.17 p.m.

Valentine's Day. There's irony for you. Oh Simon, this weekend has been so bad. And the worst of it is, I don't know why, I still don't know why. Can't figure out where I went wrong, or why, or if it was me who went wrong or if it was him – the whole thing is chaos. Before I go any further, though, I'd better keep my promise and spit out the toad in my throat (Italian expression for getting something off your chest).

Deep breath. Here I go, and here comes Toady. Well, it's like this: I no longer have a proper physical relationship with Ferdinando, and haven't since the time of my operation. That makes it – God, it's two and a half years, thirty whole months, I had no inkling till I'd written it down how long it was. In the beginning it was me: the burst cyst gave me peritonitis, you see, and I don't know whether it was a mistake of the surgeons here (my mum kept on squawking down the telephone at me not to trust them and to come back to England, and probably she was right, but it was too late by then, I couldn't have faced the journey), but anyway they slit me open like a melon, and afterwards I had this horrible pink scar running down me in bas relief, and I didn't want Ferdinando to see it, not until it had lost its colour and wormy aspect – he's so squeamish about things like that. So I fended him off and fended him off, and involuntarily, in doing so, I must have clobbered his ego at the expense of shielding mine because when finally – timidly – I began flashing my green light again it was he who no longer wanted.

Talk about hedges and barriers. Ours has now grown to such proportions that we no longer acknowledge it because to do so would be to acknowledge also the huge patch of shadow it throws on our marriage. For that reason, I think, and that reason only, we go on sleeping in the same bed, but contact between us has shrivelled to the point that if our feet so much as touch we leap apart like inverted magnets, even on the threshold of sleep. It's not very comfortable, I promise you. In fact it's agony, and eerie beyond words. And eerier still is the fact that Ferdinando (can't obviously vouch for myself but I doubt it somehow, my monitor works overtime where pride is concerned) has on three separate occasions in this two-year period, *during* sleep, when he has *crossed* the threshold, done a complete volte-face and clung to me, shuddering and whimpering like a child.

On the first occasion I responded, and then he awoke and it was ghastly. His recoil – I can't bring myself to describe it. (And I'm not beautiful, Si, but I'm not ugly either, I swear, and the scar – well, it's faded a lot, and it's only a kind of line now, and it's part of me, and . . . oh, never mind, eh. But I do, I mind dreadfully.) Anyway, the second and third times I knew better, and made no move, just lay there and waited till the crisis or nightmare or whatever it was had passed of its own accord.

Ouuf. Breathe again. There, that's the background of the picture. And if it's not very redolent of a happy union, the foreground is worse. Rows seem to blow up between us like squalls, for the stupidest reasons. Sometimes it's my clothes, my lack of what Ferdinando calls style – he's so *Italian* that way, so slavish about appearances, what people will think, what people will say. Sometimes it's something more trivial still, like the mispronunciation of a word, or the choice of a dish in a restaurant, or the fact that he wants to see one film, me another. If it weren't for the nocturnal clinging and his constant attempts to drag me back to Naples all the time, I'd think he was sick to death of me and wanted a divorce, but it's not that simple: he wants me *with* him, but on terms which for me are impossible because I don't understand what they are. Perhaps it's not even me that he wants, but some other person he'd like me to be but I can't.

This weekend it was the book again. Can you *imagine* anything more daft? The book on Fersen that I'd told him at the outset I was writing, and that he did his damnedest to discourage. I can remember more or less the exact arguments he used: You can never bring it off, he said, because you can never understand the first thing about a sensitive, tormented, guilt-ridden character like Fersen's. (Implication being that he *can*, being so much cleverer and subtler and aristocratic and whatnot. Absurd, but he sounded almost jealous: as if I was poaching on what ought by rights to be his domain.) You put him in a bottle and stick a label on: homosexual, vain, effete, artistic leanings with no talent to back them, and think you've captured his essence. Arrogance. Typical English arrogance. And English superficiality. What do you know about what really made him tick? What do you know about Capri either, for that matter? Or about the period? Nothing, you know nothing, and skimming through a few old photographs and traipsing about the island with that bloated dog of yours in tow (in fact he's quite fond of Mitzi: it was he who bought her for me, although sometimes I think more as a fetter than a pet) is not going to teach you anything either . . .

And so on and so forth till you'd have thought he'd been paid by the Fersen estate or something to get me to desist; and now, this weekend, I tell him I've stopped and am following up the Tonino thread instead, and he goes berserk. Berserk, Si, there's no other word for it: a madman, a wild, wild creature, that stares and stutters and lunges at my computer again with the intent of God knows what – wrecking it, I suppose – but luckily misses.

What *can* it matter to him what I write about? What I think about? What I do with my time when I'm here alone? I just don't get it. 'I won't have you doing this,' he screams at me, practically in falsetto, which sounds so weird coming out of his towering frame that I get the giggles, making things worse. 'Not you, not my wife. Going around like some hack journalist, playing the busybody, meddling in people's lives, upsetting their feelings, awaking painful memories, and all for what? In order to find an excuse for not living with me any more. Because that's what you want to do, isn't it? Be honest with yourself. You want to leave me, divorce me, be rid of me, forget me, take up with someone else if you haven't already . . .' Wurrawa, wurra-wa.

Then, just as suddenly as it started, the mad fit passes and he goes all limp and craven. Didn't want to say that, didn't want to hurt me, understands my need to be alone for a while and do something creative, he knows it's not easy being . . . (Pregnant pause to underline just the reverse: that I am sterile. He loves children, incidentally; children perhaps would have saved us.) *Piccolina. Topolina.* Why don't I persevere with the Fersen project? It was such a good idea, and I am in an ideal position to carry it out. Who better than me? That article he sent me? Well, no, that was just selfishness, wanting to have me back. The book under review was quite different, he'd checked, it had nothing to do with Fersen at all. Why don't I switch on the computer and show him some of the bits I've written, and he can comment on them for me. He bets they're fine, I have such an individual, quirky way of looking at things, and my famous English sense of humour . . .

Not arrogance, not superficiality any more, as my national characteristics, but sense of humour. Complete U-turn. Don't know why but the idea of him peering into my computer felt like a violation, I just couldn't face letting him do it after his manic behaviour (besides, there's nothing *on* Fersen, only the villa), so I gathered the thing in my arms, as if it were an infant or something equally precious, and backed off into the bedroom, where I hid it under the bed.

Slight madness on my side too, but then madness generates madness. How else can you react when a partner is so unpredictable, so random in his responses, so unsettling to live with, or even be with for short periods of time? They lose their balance, you lose yours; it's simple statics. And connected to this lack of balance, I've got another thing to confess, Simon, and I might as well do it now: I've been spying on him recently. Well, not really spying but . . . Well, yes, spying. He's got this mobile phone, you see, like all Italians have, with an answer service that clicks in when he's not using it; and at nights, when he's asleep and I know the thing's switched off, I've been trying to crack the code and get at his messages. Only four numbers, so it didn't take long, because his memory's dreadful and I knew it would be something to do with his birth date, and it was.

Simon, I *know*. You don't have to say anything. It goes SO MUCH AGAINST THE GRAIN with me, this snooping, and I am so bitterly, bitterly ashamed, that I won't ever do it again. It served no purpose anyway: the only women's voices (because, yes, I know he's got someone else, he must have, he used to get headaches in the past, like Kennedy, when he skipped a day, he must have) the only women's voices were Matilde's, ordering him to get special orange-flower essence for a cake she wants to make for Easter, and a wheedly, peasanty-sounding lady with a strong local accent, speaking to the answer service as if it was a person, asking for the *Dottore. Grazie, Signorina*, sorry to bother you, I'll call back tomorrow, it was just I wanted to remind the *Dottore* about . . . he knows what. *Scusi. Grazie. Scusi.* Probably someone he's keeping up his sleeve to fill the next vacancy on Matilde's staff: she goes through domestics like a pin through balloons, bursting them as she goes.

Oh Christ, what a mess I've landed myself in, what a trap. If it weren't for Mitzi, I swear I'd have packed my bags and been back in England by now, but I've got to sit it out until March at least when the quarantine laws are repealed. Roll on March 1st, or is it April?

Then perhaps we could meet, Si? What do you say? Have a meal somewhere and laugh about all this silly, chilly winter that'll seem years away by then. Hopefully. Do you like champagne? I love the stuff. I will stand you a huge jeroboam (why doesn't my computer like this word? It suggests jerboa instead, which is a jumping rodent and not what I want to present you with at all) for being so sweet and patient and listening to this blooming jeremiad.

Jeroboam, jumping jerboa, jeremiad – my usual pitfall. *Baci*, which besides being kisses are also delicious chocolates, box of which I will send you by and by. L.

From: salvia@libero.it
To: sparks@bookhound.com
Subject: maybe taboo and best left alone?
Date: Wed, Feb 16, 2000, 8.20 p.m.

Si, you know that warning that crops up on the Internet when you've been using it for a long stretch: 'X Your Life is dangerously boring.' Well, I'm afraid it must apply to you if you really want me to go on writing you all these yards of messages. Either that or (something I already suspected) you are too darn nice for your own good.

You *can't* really want to know about Matilde: nobody does. I'm not going to inflict her on you anyway. Today I have far more interesting things to tell you. Yesterday Nico and I, in great secret, crammed on our deerstalkers and took the hydrofoil to Naples, where we did various things:

– bought Greek yoghurt for our next tacos (but that's not *very* interesting, I grant).

– bought two simply GRIPPING books on paedophiles and victims of. Much easier than the Freud, less theory and more practice, intended for an altogether more earthbound readership, like social workers and plodding *poliziotti* and ourselves. Discovered, from the bookshop we bought them in, the existence of a Neapolitan Sexology Association that holds lectures once a week on all sorts of connected themes, and booked ourselves in to '*Parafilie Varie*' by Dottoressa A. Trombetta (which sends Nico into hysterics, *tromba* being a rather peculiar word in Italian in the context) in two weeks' time. We are told *parafilia* is a blanket term and covers paedophilia and MUCH ELSE BESIDES, so I hope to emerge from under the blanket an all-round wiser woman.

– had a delicious fishy lunch

and now comes the really interesting part

– met up with Augusta Esposito, the young deputy teacher who stood in for Tonino's regular class mistress for three whole months the winter he died. It was a – I don't know how to describe it, I suppose you could call it a profitable meeting from the point of view of fact finding, if profit didn't sound so wrong in the circumstances. We took to each other straightaway, all three of us, and we spoke for ages and ages – missing boat after boat. Poor girl, I think she was glad to have someone – anyone – to confide in. Nico (sceptical. Like you, I think: admit it) had so far accompanied me on this quest out of kindness: because he thought it was good for me to have something to think about that wasn't my own wretched marital embroilments. But the longer we spoke, and the more things Augusta revealed, the more I could see him getting won over to my theory, and now, just as I'm starting to get cold feet about the whole thing and wanting to stop and have a think before we go any further (because what do I *do* with my famous patch of damp if I actually find it, eh? Call in the damp experts – whoever they might be? Or plaster it over again and try to forget about it? Certainly can't use a story like this for copy if it's real), he's ranting at me that we must forge ahead, do more, find out more, no matter what.

This morning he was round already, waving one of our new textbooks at me in which he'd underlined the parts that corresponded with what Augusta had told us. And I must say, the fit is uncanny; to see it there in black and white (and yellow – the marker he has used is bright lemon yellow) gives me a kind of tingly feeling in my blood, as if I was a scientist standing on the brink of some new discovery. See if it doesn't hit you that way too.

Augusta admits she doesn't have much experience, it was only her second posting, but she says she's sure, and was fairly sure at the time even, that poor little Tonino had some big problem hanging over him. To the point that when she'd heard of the accident her first thought had been that he'd committed suicide. The doubt had never quite left her, either, nor the sense of possibly having failed him; she tried not to think of it but she dreamed of it sometimes. Him drowning, her trying to reach him underwater, grabbing hold of his jersey, it unravelling in her hand – things like that.

What kind of problem, we asked? Big, she said, unmanageably big for a ten-year-old. Like drugs, or debts (yes, debts can be run up at that age, it's quite common, especially here in Naples), or bullying, or troubles of some kind at home. He showed all the signs they'd always been told to look out for in teaching college: restlessness, apathy, aggressive behaviour with the other children, inability to concentrate – trouble was, they were signs of common or garden naughtiness as well. She'd brought the matter up with the other teachers, but they wouldn't listen, treated her like an over-zealous novice. It was difficult that way when you were temporary – you had to be careful not to put people's backs up, or instead of helping you they did the opposite.

So what else had she done? What else had she tried to do? The *bidella* said she'd taken pains over Tonino. How? In what way? Well, looking back on it, obviously not in the right way, she said. She'd sent notes via him to the parents, asking for them to come and talk things over with her, but no one had ever come, and she hadn't followed up this idea by going to talk to them herself because Tonino had seemed so set against it. It seemed to rock him, rob him of his balance. If you could speak of balance, because that was what he was lacking really, all round. He used to have these wild mood swings: one minute he'd be leaping round the classroom, baiting the other children and jogging their elbows and snatching their copybooks away and generally playing the nuisance – he was quite funny when he did that, and the others put up with it surprisingly well – and the next he'd slump down at his desk, almost lifeless, like a toy when its battery's given out. He had age swings too: sometimes you'd think he was practically an adult – he could flirt, he could be chivalrous, he could be cynical, all things far ahead of his years – and at other times he could be downright babyish. When she'd wanted to contact the family, for example, he'd clung to her like a little monkey and begged her, quite, quite seriously, to become his mother instead so that he could leave home and come and live with her. A child of ten – nearly eleven – knows this is impossible and accepts it, but Tonino no, he'd thrown a gigantic tantrum; kicked her, punched her, as if it was her fault she couldn't change his parentage. And yet it wasn't as if he didn't know the facts of life. They all knew those, all the class: some of the jokes that went round . . . worse than a barracks.

Had she ever brought him home with her, made a fuss of him, done anything special with him? Not really, she said. She looked miserable when she said that. The instability had unnerved her: she'd been afraid of worsening it. The time he'd had ringworm and all those bald patches had appeared on his head – she'd taken him to the cinema then, with four other kids, to cheer him up a bit, but that was about it. And once they'd gone to the hot springs on Ischia for a picnic, but that had been a class outing. Otherwise, no, she'd just tried, like you do with a nervy horse, to reassure him by being patient with him, treating him gently, dedicating a bit more time to him in class than the others. Her father was a vet: you got horses in Naples sometimes – racehorses, thoroughbreds – cooped up in garages, in the dark, and let out only on race days. Problem horses, they became. Victims of ignorance and wrong handling.

And Tonino had definitely been wrong handled by someone, in her view. Probably the father, she'd always thought, but nothing had come out, not even at the time of the inquest. Accident. OK, probably was, almost certainly was, but there'd been those drawings of his, for instance – those really violent drawings, all black and splotches and scribbles – and nobody had listened to her, nobody had wanted to see them, nobody had paid any attention at all. The child couldn't draw, so what? Just showed how backward he was. *And* clumsy. Explained why he fell.

The drawing thing intrigued us. We asked if she'd kept

any, so that we could have a look. No, she said. Maybe she should have done, as a memento, but they weren't the sort of drawings anybody'd want to keep – they were just scrawls really. Angry, childish scrawls. Where would they be now? What would have become of them? They'd have been thrown away at the end of term with all the others. Unless the parents had come to claim them, which she thought unlikely. What were they of? Oh, aeroplanes mostly – missiles, aeroplanes, rockets with smoke and flames coming out of them – typical boy stuff. It wasn't the subject that had struck her, no, so much as the way he'd tackled it: harsh lines, dark colours, underscoring so heavy that it tore the paper in places. (Nico's eyebrows went up at this point and stayed up.)

And his school work? Same thing. The police hadn't had any use for that either, only in that case they were right: there was nothing there to prove that he was unhappy or stressed in any way, except the things that were missing. You'd give them a *tema*, a composition: My Favourite Hobby; My Christmas Hols; and he'd either skip it altogether, or else he'd do something so thin and stilted there'd be no ring of truth in it at all. You could usually pick up things about children's backgrounds that way – little things they let slip. Boozy fathers, bullying elder brothers, flighty mums. Tonino, no, he was zipped up as tight as an Arctic explorer in a tent. But there again, it was nothing you could put a finger on, nothing you could bring up with the other teachers to convince them. He had no *fantasia*, that was all they said when she mentioned it, no imagination.

Poor little Tonino, I shall be having dreams about him soon, too. My thwarted breeding instincts etc.; the son I never had. That little photo on the headstone – I half wish I'd never seen it, then at least I wouldn't have a face to attach to the name.

And now – help, it's late, no wonder Mitzi is bashing me for her dinner – here come Nico's underlinings in the paedo handbook, taken from a list of hallmarks of abused children:

- poor performance at school
- poor peer-group relationships
- aggressiveness
- hyperactivity
- lethargy
- truancy
- introversion
- regressive behaviour
- unsuitably adult behaviour
- attempts at flight from home, or fantasies of adoption by other parents
- suicide attempts

There. What do you say to that? The list is much longer of course, nineteen items in all, and several things, like bed-wetting and headaches and eating disorders and hypochondria and so forth, we're not in a position to know, nor probably ever will be, but even so the congruence is extraordinary – well over 50 per cent. And not only that, but another of the signals I haven't included is alopecia – loss of hair – bald patches – and Nico says, and I don't think it's *that* far-fetched either, that what Augusta called ringworm might easily have been that: alopecia. It's a typical psychosomatic reaction to stress, apparently.

OK, that may be pushing it slightly, I admit – warping the evidence to fit the theory. But then there's the *drawings*. The book shows whole pages of drawings by abused children of all ages, and, Simon – well, it's easy to imagine, isn't it? Not always rockets and missiles, sometimes houses, sometimes chimneys, sometimes people, sometimes snakes, but all of them, without exception, in that threatening upright phallic shape, and nearly all of them displaying some kind of terminal explosion or emission. Oh God, makes you wince.

Can it be just coincidence? At this point I think not. The fall may be unconnected of course, and in any case a connection would be almost impossible to establish, especially after all this time, but I'm quite certain, and so is Nico now, that Tonino was the victim of abuse. Sexual abuse, I mean. On the part of someone. Although who – father, relative, elder school companion or just some chance acquaintance – we shall probably never know.

Nico is anxious for us to make at least one visit to the family, just to see what they're like and what comes of it. He's pretty sure it won't get us anywhere, save possibly into trouble, and he admits the idea scares him silly, but he thinks it's our duty to try. My own instinct is to follow Ferdinando's counsel, who after all knows the islanders much better than we do, and pack it in, and let ill alone. It's not as if we could help the poor little boy any more, and conceivably we could do a lot of harm.

WHAT IS YOUR OPINION, SI, AS AN IMPARTIAL OUTSIDER? DOES THE ABUSE THEORY CONVINCE YOU OR DO YOU THINK NICO AND I ARE LETTING OUR IMAGINATIONS RUN AWAY WITH US? AND IF

BY ANY CHANCE YOU *ARE* CONVINCED, WHAT IS THE NEXT STEP? FORWARDS OR BACKWARDS?

Please be quick in replying because I'm getting into a bit of a state about the whole thing, and really don't know what is best, L.

From: salvia@libero.it
To: sparks@bookhound.com
Subject: matters to me, urgently
Date: Fri, Feb 18, 2000, 11.33 a.m.

No egg. No message. Expect you're busy, never mind, eh. Just as long as when it arrives it is a helpful one. I really do need your advice about this business, Si, it's preying on my mind no end. I daren't ask Ferdinando after the scene he made last time, in fact I daren't bring up with him the topic of my writing at all: for some reason it's a minefield – one wrong step and Splatter. Nico is hopeless, he's like a Yorkshire terrier on the tracks of a rat, all barks and rushes and false starts and doublings home again, I wish I'd never told him. And Mitzi's cut her paw and my mum's just rung to say she's got shingles and the cleaning lady's off work (mine, I mean, not hers) and Matilde's threatening a visit over Easter and a huge bill's blown in from the accountant and Friday's come around again too. Horrorbins. L.

PS I never answered your question about adoption, but the answer is no. We're neither of us generous enough. F would never want a child that wasn't his, unless by some fluke it looked exactly like him. And I wouldn't be confident enough of my own heart to go it alone.

PPS Unless the child in question looked exactly like Tonino, in which case . . . Oh what a shame it all is: if I were God, there are a few loose ends I think I would have tied up tighter.

From: salvia@libero.it
To: sparks@bookhound.com
Subject: matters more urgently still
Date: Fri, Feb 18, 2000, 7.43 p.m.

Still no reply. If you're thinking of sending one over the weekend, please don't, not until Monday. Afternoon to be safe. When I opened my computer this evening the list of recent docs showed different files from the ones I've been using and I have a vague suspicion Ferdinando has been fiddling with it. Nothing strange in that – he does use it sometimes when he's here – except that when I asked him he got angry with me again and denied it. I don't mind him reading my pathetic literary efforts, not really, provided he stays on his rocker about them, but I do mind him peering into my e-mail. Xxxs in haste, L.

From: salvia@libero.it
To: sparks@bookhound.com
Subject: of ever more urgent inquiry
Date: Mon, Feb 21, 2000, 5.46 p.m.

_____

S ???? L.

From: salvia@libero.it
To: sparks@bookhound.com
Subject: to a sudden change of mind
Date: Mon, Feb 21, 2000, 6.54 p.m.

Forgive my fidgets, Si, I forget there's an hour's difference. I thought, God, he's left the office already and now I'll have to wait till tomorrow at least.

Vada avanti, you say in your best Italian, meaning go for it. No, no mistake, only with the grade of intimacy we've achieved, it would be better to say *Va avanti*, or *Vai avanti*, 2nd pers sing.

Oh Christ, in a way I'm relieved, in a way I'm not. I'm relieved you too think there's something in this story that needs looking into, but not relieved you think I'm the one who ought to do it. I've been to the outside of the parents' house already this morning, and it's not at all inviting, I assure you. It's not that far from here (well, nowhere is far on this weenzie island, but I mean it's not far in strictly Capri terms either). You take the road to Villa Fersen – the creepy road I don't like – and about three-quarters of the way along you get to a wildish area with lots of scrub, dotted by a few very small smallholdings, and it's one of those. The house stands alone, quite high up, off the path, and it looks pretty run-down from the outside. Scurvy chickens, a chained-up dog that went into a frenzy at the sight of Mitzi, the wreck of a scooter, a wire fence and a gate made of bedsprings – just to give you the general idea. Were it not for the animals, and a certain watchfulness about the shutters, as if there was someone behind them peering out at you, you might easily take it for unlived-in. I don't really want to drag Nico there – I need someone less flappable – but I don't think I could face walking up that path all on my own and knocking on the door.

In fact I don't think I can face it full stop. What on earth could I say to whoever opened it? I'm a spoilt, bored Englishwoman who's thought up a theory in her spare time about your son having committed suicide and wants to check it out? Is your husband around? Oh well, never mind, perhaps you can tell me: Did he by any chance molest his son – in a sexual way, you know – bad enough to drive him off the top of a cliff? Or did some other member of your family? An uncle maybe? Or wicked old Grandad?

No, I know, I'm being silly, of course there are subtler ways of doing it, but even so . . . No, I funk it, Si. I'm stopping here. Nico can do what he likes, but I'm calling a halt to the whole lunatic business. I'm not cut out for detective work – real *or* imaginary. I'm dumping the thriller too, if I write anything at all I'm going to follow Ferdinando's advice and go back to Fersen. Maybe, I don't know, a straight biography or something. Any news, incidentally, on those two books? The ones I ordered to begin with? Keep putting out feelers, won't you, they'd be dead useful when I start.

If I start. Because from tomorrow I'm taking a break, and then we shall see. Ferdinando is going to Tuscany on a scout-around for antiques, and he's persuaded me to go with him, leaving Mitzi in the care of Nico. Things were so much better between us this weekend, he was so much kinder and friendlier and more relaxed, hardly lost his temper at all, except the once, over the business of the computer (which I think I was wrong about anyway: it has behaved a bit oddly several times since it fell). Bought me a bracelet, brought me breakfast in bed, remembered to buy me a fresh copy of *The Times* in Naples and then sat on the bed and wrote silly messages to me in the columns of the crossword. You say I'm jealous of him and must therefore be still in love with him. I don't know if either of these statements is true, I only know that seeing him like this – approachable, attentive, the protective coating he's worn recently coming apart at the seams a bit and patches of his old sweet self showing through – I thought it would be selfish and wrong of me not to respond. Seven or eight days – surely I can spare that amount of time for him. For our marriage. It's not as if . . .

Well, you know how darned busy I am, don't you, who better? And you know too to what profitable account I've turned these weeks of solitude. A pile of scattered notes, three pages of drivel, and a half-baked theory that if it's false is useless and if it's true is *worse* than useless, and that anyway doesn't concern me but none the less rattles me and gives me a permanent fluttery feeling inside – half tension, half nausea. It used to be called having butterflies in your stomach, but there's no joy or colour to the ones I have, they are more like moths.

Sorry, mate, if I am up to my old tricks again: clamouring for your advice and then, when it comes, going ahead and doing the exact opposite, but that's partly why I find it so important to write to you. It clears my head. I wonder if you

71

find that too with the written word? I set down in print whatever muddle it is that's flummoxing me, and abracadabra, after a few hours, or sometimes less, it has sorted itself out. Enough, at least, to enable me to see the strands and where they lead. (And the Tonino strand, believe me, goes nowhere, nowhere, nowhere.)

I'm sorry too that we shall lose our main topic of conversation now, but I don't somehow think this will bother us, do you? There's always your dramas to fall back on (you haven't told me how the row over the peppermints ended, for one), and if we get desperate there's always Matilde. I shall close for a while, because I'm not taking the computer with me, but at the beginning of March at the latest I will be back. Hopefully to tell you that all is HUNKY-DORY (now where did that one come from, you clever old entomologist?), and that Ferdinando and I have put on our gardening gloves and not only clipped and pruned but actually uprooted our dratted hedge and replaced it with a charming little border of love-in-a-mist. Some hope! Meanwhile much love to you in a bank of rather threatening cloud – Lola.

From: salvia@libero.it
To: sparks@bookhound.com
Subject: to no one's caprices any more
Date: Fri, Feb 25, 2000, 5.43 p.m.

Hiya, Sparky, here I am, back already. The trip was a disaster. Or perhaps it wasn't, perhaps it was only a disaster in my stupid imagination. If I made a Ruth Rendall out of the Tonino story, I made a frigging Barbara Cartland out of my own, and of course, if anything literary, it's closer to Pinter. Middle-class matrimonial mincemeat. I wouldn't dare admit this to anyone else, not even to Althea, who would kill me for my gormlessness, but on the day we set out I went and bought myself a glamorous new nightie, hoping against all reason and experience for a *rapprochement* on the physical plane. Can you imagine anything more pathetic? A bullet-proof vest would have been more suitable.

Oh Simon, why does he want me with him if he doesn't want me? And I don't mean only sex. I know I was in the way, I felt it all the time. I'm not difficult to be with, I'm not bad company, I'm not boring – I say this quite objectively, or as objectively as I can, being naturally a titch biased in my own favour. I travel well, I don't complain, I'm not carsick, I'm amenable to any suggestions. Let's stop here

73

and I stop, let's eat that and I eat it, let's do that and I do it. I'm not moody – *he's* the moody one. I'm not obstreperous either. And then I was so *happy*, so optimistic, so looking forward to it all. And I'm at my best when I'm happy, everyone is, and my best is really quite good.

It's a nightmare. It's not as if I was lacking in critical sense either, but I just don't know *what* I do *wrong*. I set his teeth on edge – my mere presence does – I can see it, I can feel it, even a rhino could through all its hide. But if this is so, then WHY THE FUCK (not a well-chosen word in the circumstances) did he want me along with him? Answer this if you can. And no, it's got nothing to do with weepiness or victimisation or emotional blackmail, because I avoid all these like the plague. I'm not a victim, I never have been and I don't want to become one. Apart from the nightie, which I don't think he even noticed, I didn't drop any hints at all, didn't put on any pressure, didn't show any signs of expectation when we bedded down together at night in the various hotels along the route, or any signs of disappointment when he turned his back on me with what was almost, I swear, last night at least, a shudder. I was just there – in line with *his* suggestion, not mine. And he was just elsewhere.

Why should I lie there in hostile darkness to be shuddered at? Why should I sit at table with him and watch him twitching with impatience, waiting for the moment when he can decently dump me and go off and make a secret telephone call to some other woman in whose company he'd rather be? I won't, I didn't. This morning, while he was at breakfast, I simply packed my things and called a cab and went to the station, and now here I am, back in my cosy crow's nest with my Mitzi and my computer and the prospect of a good few Ferdinando-free days ahead. The evening is unbelievable. From the main terrace, did I ever tell you, I can see the sun setting in a huge pink pool behind Monte Solaro, and from the rear one I can see plumb down to Punta di Massullo: opals on one side, streaked with fire, sapphires and emeralds on the other. What more do I want?

If the split with Ferdinando becomes definite, I think I might buy this villa off the family and go on living here. Three or four months a year, sort of thing. Then you could come and stay, Si, if I haven't frightened you off with all this show of emotion.

Which, I repeat and beg you to believe, is utterly foreign to me. Or has been until now. There'd be nothing to be ashamed of if I was, in fact I think I'd be rather proud of it, but I'm *not* an emotional person, and that is the truth. I'm calm, stable, don't think I've made a scene since I was christened, if then – I must ask my mum. All these mysterious undercurrents that lap about me recently, and that I'm pretty damned sure I've done nothing to create, are twisting me into a shape that is not my own.

Do you think I ought to see a shrink? Wonder if Capri boasts one? Did you ever go to one yourself in time of trouble? Oh piss it all, I'm fed up with not being happy, it's not my nature. Why should I bother myself any more with cures or rescues? Ferdinando's the one who's in the shit pit, let him climb out on his own. Separation, divorce, solitude, staying on in Italy, returning to England, beginning life all over again – it's all fine by me. In fact I look forward to *anything* that's not this slow brand of torture I go through when I'm with him. I think I called it the Torquemada Twostep to you in an earlier letter, but that implies connivance – two to tango etc. If I've been guilty of collaboration in the past, or of passivity at the very least, I won't be any more. Signed on behalf of the LLF, the Lola Liberation Front.

And now I must stop and go and do some last-minute shopping. I have Nico coming to supper. He says he's got things to tell me. My heart sinks a bit at the way he says _Things_, because I foresee either love troubles or else more dotty conjectures regarding Tonino, and quite honestly I've had my fill of both topics for the time being.

When you write, please tell me all about the new films you're seeing and the new books you're reading and the rocks new you're climbing. I want a fresh breeze through my brain. Best love, Lola.

From: salvia@libero.it
To: sparks@bookhound.com
Subject: you find difficult to broach
Date: Sun, Feb 27, 2000, 2.28 p.m.

Oh Si, I'm sorry. That makes two of us. (And three with Nico, whose partner is apparently threatening to come back from America shortly with a new love and hoof him out of the villa. What a fortunate trio we do make.) But if she didn't appreciate you then she must have been unworthy. Niceness *shines* through your letters. And not only niceness, which sounds a bit deadly on its own, I always think, but fascination too. Perhaps you're one of those people who will have to wait a while before finding a soulmate: catch a thirty-plus-year-old, rather like me, who went for the icing on the cake first and is now repenting and looking for good wholesome flourmix. I'm sure someone like that will come along, it's just a question of believing and not getting downcast in the interval. When you're young the breeding instinct fouls you up in your choices, I think that's what it is. A few bright feathers and a sexy warble, and you're lost. Look at me and Ferdinando: I *never* should have married him. I should have been more scientific: got my binoculars out and watched him, made a list of his haunts, his habits, seen what he was like before mealtimes when aggressiveness is highest, noted how he responded to danger, whether he was a panicker or a planner, fundamental things like that. Taken a good dekko at his old hen-bird mum too while I was about it. *Think* if I'd had children and they had taken after her! Now I'd be ringed round by cuckoos.

Quite honestly I've had reservations about your lady ever since the Great Polomint Drama: anyone who makes that amount of fuss over such a small fault – if fault indeed it be to harbour fluff-coated mints about one's person, and this needs first establishing – is, let's face it, not going to make a tolerant partner ever. In fact I'd like to go one step further and say that to me she sounds dangerously mad, but these are early days and there is always the risk you will hitch up with her again, and then I will be placed in the uncomfortable position of having to retract.

Ah well, never mind, eh. (You ask why I repeat this so often. It's a refrain from childhood, a family joke whose origins are forgotten. Who used to say it? Why? No idea, all I know is that for some silly reason it still makes me laugh. The stress goes on the eh, and the overall pronunciation, should it interest you, is Never Mine *Day*.) When did I write my first letter to you? Somewhere in the middle of Jan, I think. And what are we now? Coming up end of Feb. Six whole weeks and now here I am back exactly where I started: on Capri, on my total tod, in full matrimonial shipwreck, and no useful idea to work on and take my mind off things except the abandoned Fersen project. Alluring as last week's lasagne.

I can't go along with Nico, I really can't. I'd miss him dreadfully, but in a way it'd be a good thing if the boyfriend evicted him. I want to forget about the Tonino business entirely. I know I was the one who started it, but by the same token I should be the one to end it, no? if I feel so inclined. There's a real tragedy there, a real boy, a real death, I feel it's wrong to monkey around with it like we've been doing. Because, yes, let's face it, that's all we've been doing: monkeying around. If the fall from the cliff was an accident, then investigation is mere gratuitous prying, and if it wasn't . . . If it wasn't, well then there's another grave human drama underlying the event, but one so intimate and complicated that we, as outsiders, have no justification in seeking to uncover it. I've been back to the cemetery to look at the photograph – commune a little with Tonino in my head, tune myself to his wavelength and see if I can't pick up some silent echoes – and all that the little face seems to say to me is, I'm dead, Lola, you can't help me now.

Nico, blast him, is still in the game stage. You know what he's gone and done while I was away? He's been padding around making a nuisance of himself, accosting more people, asking more questions. He's been to the registry office, looking for the death certificate (which told him nothing, I knew it wouldn't). He's tried to get hold of the doctor who signed it, and has been cordially told to go to blazes. He's been to the house – the one I described to you – and has found out it doesn't belong to the Vicos any more: they've sold it recently and moved to the mainland, where Tonino's father has started up a hire-car company. This Nico needless to say interprets as a sinister sign, indicating that the family has come into money, and that the money is hush money . . . Etc., etc., I really can't bear to listen to him.

We had quite a row about it when he came to supper. From the gay network, whose feelers reach all sorts of places here on Capri, public and private, official and non, he has somehow managed to pick up a rumour of allegedly 'insider' stamp about the condition in which Tonino's body was found, and I had to actually put my fingers in my ears and shout streams of gibberish to prevent myself from hearing. Every time I stopped he started again, and in the end I got so angry I barricaded myself in the bedroom and turned the telly on loud and didn't come out until I'd obtained a solemn oath from him, sworn on his mother's cranium, who's always having migraines, that he'd shut up. He just didn't seem able to take my point, which was that, true or not, probable or improbable, reliable or un- in its credentials, I SIMPLY DID NOT WANT TO HEAR IT.

Result: instead of two friends to talk to daily and download my problems on, I now have one – yourself.

And now, before I close, a quick survey of the money question. No, I don't take offence about your bringing it up, not a bit. Sometimes I've even thought it myself: the Acquaviva family fortunes going down the drain, as they have been steadily for the last four generations, and me a convenient plug to stop the flow. I don't have a high enough opinion of myself to rule it out entirely. On the other hand I don't have a low enough opinion to *credit* it entirely. Motives are always tangled, aren't they, always difficult to separate? So I would answer your query thus: money may have been one of Ferdinando's motives in marrying me to start with, but I don't somehow think it's one of the motives that stops him wanting to leave me now. For one thing, I've spent a lot of money already on doing up the various Acquaviva properties, so if that particular goal was what he had in mind, he's achieved it, and it's a lasting one. For another, his own financial situation has improved a good deal since our marriage, and so has Matilde's, who inherited quite a lot of land last year from a virtually *immortal* old uncle, and has now sold it off for building lots. Neither of them has offered to repay me my outlay, mind you, but neither of them is dependent on my income any more. What bills do I go on footing? Well, I'm not sure, I'd have to ask the accountant, but I think the present position is that I'm responsible only for my own clothes and household expenses and for the upkeep of that part of the palazzo in Naples in which I (normally) live together with Ferdinando. And that's all. While I'm here on Capri I pay whatever bills come in here too, but I have no quarrel with that – after all, I'm the one who's using the place. Ferdinando is very proud and touchy about money: this makes it difficult to talk to him on the subject, and for the same reason he hates me quizzing the accountant too closely, who is a friend of his from university days. It may even be that he's settling the Naples bills himself nowadays; I shall try, discreetly, to work it out. Although, as I say, I *don't* think this area is where the crux of the matter lies.

There, have I calmed your fears on this account? Don't *worry* about me, Si. I get a bit theatrical now and again when I'm low, but basically what am I? A lucky, pampered richbitch, that is what: youngish, strongish, healthy, leading a lazy tranquil life in one of the most beautiful spots on the entire globe, and whose only worries are: 1) a slightly neurotic and andropausal husband who's gone off her a bit, and 2) the fact that she can't think up a good subject to write about and counteract the occasional fits of blues to which she is prone.

Re your poetical thoughts on Feb – no, I don't like the *promise* of spring at all, I like it when it actually delivers the goods. Which it already has here, more or less, aren't you envious? By the way, I have half an idea of coming to

London before long, if I can find a sitter for Mitzi. (Burnt my chances with Nico, but I couldn't have asked him anyway, not twice running.) Can we meet, do you think? Should we risk it? Or should we play safe and go on as we are? What if we take one look and . . . horrorbins? Then it would be all over between our virtual selves as well.

Mull all this over in your well-equipped noddle. And write soon. You can probably tell from the slightly feverish tone of this message that I am once more unsettled inside. I never should have left base. Never mine day, yr fond and foolish friend, Lola. (Not so foolish, however, as not to know what an entomologist is. That, *mein schulmeistery Schatz*, was just a little *choke*.)

From: salvia@libero.it
To: sparks@bookhound.com
Subject: catalogue
Date: Tue, Feb 29, 2000, 9.15 p.m.

Thanks for the lecture. (Blast, I was forgetting, got another one coming tomorrow: Trombetta. Patched it up with Nico and he's coming to fetch me and we're going together. Such knowledge as we acquire will come in handy for the Fersen book – more about that in a sec.) You're dead right, for people in our plight work is essential, and the last two days I've done nothing but. *Et tu, Brute?* (More brackets, but you know the first time I came across this quote in Shakespeare I thought it was French, and did so for ages. No, this time no joke, merely a humble confession.) I've read my way through everything I could lay my hands on . . .

Incidentally, nimbly avoiding a third pair of brackets, is either of those books you're after *ever* going to show up, do you think, or should I abandon hope? I've tried the Internet, several times, but all I got for Fersen was Marie Antoinette, and all I got for Peyrefitte was a whole lot of stuff on Alexander the Great and foot fetishists. Why should this be so? And what could possibly be the *raison d'être* for an Alexander the Great knitting circle?

83

. . . which amounts to two long biographical essays in English and one immensely detailed but whimsical book in Italian about Fersen's will and things, giving the full inventory of the villa, not quite as made by the coroner at the time of the funeral, who apparently jumbled everything up in one long list, but painstakingly regrouped in the author's imagination, room by room, object by object.

Makes grotty, Ludwigian reading, just as I thought, but perhaps so would the detailed contents of anybody's house: dreadful mishmash of styles – Chinese, Roman, Louis XV, art nouveau; deluge of knick-knacks – fauns and nymphs and *putti* in great preponderance; screens, cushions, kimonos, swathes of material, often pink in colour; and to top it all two huge paintings of the principal boyfriend, Nino Cesarini, one demurely clothed in pinstripe jacket, and one *desnudo*, sitting bareback astride a rearing white charger, a red cloak grazing the shoulders and fluttering away behind him in the wind.

So anyway, as far as groundwork is concerned I've made a start. One big Brownie point in my favour. And as far as Ferdinando is concerned I've made a stop. Two big Brownie points. Today, Feb 29th, is his birthday – his proper birthday, his twelfth – and falling on this millennium date it has a special significance apparently, but have I rung him on his mobile to wish him happy returns and try to make up our quarrel? I have not. I have kept utter silence since I sneaked out of the hotel on Friday morning, and so has he – not even a tinkle to sound out where I am and if I arrived safely – and I reckon that more or less sets the black waxen seal of closure on our relationship. *FINIS*. All sorts of emotions bob about inside me as a result, but the only one I can identify, it being much the strongest, is relief. (And no, I haven't been spying again either. Whoever she is, she's welcome to him.)

The switchback ride is over. Thank God for that. No Easter calvary, either, being nice to Matilde for Ferdinando's sake and having to listen to her personal history of Fascist conquest – Ciano ensnared, Grandi reduced to jelly, Mussolini's entire cabinet at her feet by the sound of it, don't believe a *word* – and play cards with her till I drop, and feed that repulsive pug of hers and clean up its dribble and shut Mitzi away to prevent her from devouring the little brute, and soothe the cleaning lady who's bound to give notice under the strain, and try and persuade her to stay on at least . . .

Oh freedom – worth paying almost any price for, don't you agree? In your case you can now harbour peppermints wherever you choose. I hope you are doing just this: stashing them away all over the place and making an Up Yours sign as you stash.

And talking of Mitzi, this afternoon I have an appointment with the vet to equip her with a microchip or whatever is needed to make her eligible for ENTRY TO BRITAIN. Probably take months, knowing how things work here, or don't work, but anyway it's a step in the right direction (i.e. north-north-west, as far away from Ferdinando as poss), and it makes me feel very resolute and adult and independent. My life a bit in tatters, maybe, but at least I'm taking the tatters into my own hands. Who knows, with a bit of thread and a bit of perseverance I may yet cobble them back into some kind of shape. Yr positive-thinking (now there's a nice grisly term for your collection), and finally positive-acting as well, e-pen-pal, Lola.

From: salvia@libero.it
To: sparks@bookhound.com
Subject: a very sensitive one
Date: Thu, Mar 2, 2000, 5.53 p.m.

I see, I see, so *that's* the link with knitting: my server wasn't working properly or I'd have found the site myself. How unsophisticated I am. And Peyrefitte = pair of feet, I suppose? Ha.

So many things I know nothing about. The lecture, Si, though badly structured and worse delivered – because the *Dottoressa*, bless her, is a wee shy mouse who lisps – was a REVELATION. Did you know that the paedophile is the most recalcitrant type of criminal there is? That there are very few instances of such people confessing to being in the grip of paedophilia, and still fewer of people who are in the grip wanting to get out of it? Doesn't this strike you as strange? Almost unbelievable? Don't you think that if you found yourself fantasising about children in that way (and it always starts in the head apparently, as fantasy), your first reaction would be to run to a psychiatrist and beg him to cure you, or even lock you up, before you went and inflicted harm on an innocent fellow creature? One miserable little firework – a one-bang squib, a fizzled rocket, for that's all an orgasm amounts to – at the cost of a child's future? I may flatter myself, and women are probably naturally more protective of the young anyway (v few lady paedos around – 5% to 95% male), but I think, even if I were a man, I'd rather be castrated than give in to such a ruthless impulse, I honestly do.

But then you never know. The whole topic is so riddled with ambiguity. Trombetta told us (serenely, not batting a mouse's eyelid) about a case she'd followed as a student, in which the mother of an eighteen-month-old baby went into the bathroom to find her husband, who was changing the baby's nappy, in state of full erection.

What would you have done if you'd been him, discovering yourself getting a hard-on under such circumstances? Broken down, no? Confessed, begged for help, anything to protect your child against this menace which, alas for all concerned, happened to be you, the child's father? And what would you have done if you had been her, the mother? Made the most terrible rumpus, of course, gone into the matter, delved, had no peace until you'd winkled out the truth, no matter how ghastly, and saved your baby from this perilous nutter. Instead, no: Father goes on unimpeded in the following years to fulfil his overriding ambition of raping Junior and ruining him for life, and Mother wipes the scene clean out of her mind and doesn't 'remember' until circumstances – like the child's breakdown and her husband's arrest and imprisonment – force her to do so. Seems totally crazy to me. Forget a scene like that? How can you forget it? OK, the human psyche is wily about shielding itself from unwanted information, but not to that extent, surely? Not to the extent of sacrificing your own beloved child?

And yet Trombetta says you see it again and again.

Mothers who 'overlook' little details like masturbation over Harry Potter (or perhaps even Beatrix) in their partners and bruised genitals in their offspring, who won't listen, won't pick up clues, who sit there like the three monkeys all rolled into one, with eyes and ears and mouth tight shut: it is not happening, not to me, not in my family, not in my marriage. In fact she says the woman in the above case was unusual inasmuch as she did finally cave in and admit to a certain degree of lateral knowledge: the opposite is more frequent, apparently, with the mother organising a last-ditch stand and accusing the child of lying and/or instigating the seduction. Stand in which, more bewilderingly still, the victim often fights side by side with the accuser, since in the long run, says T, it is less painful to believe you have *done* a great wrong rather than to have suffered one. Especially at the hands of someone you trusted absolutely.

Can you credit it? Can you take it in? I admit I scarcely can myself: I feel my brain kind of stretching, and creaking under the strain almost to snapping point. But then I think back on the Tonino story – the death no one wants to talk about, the parents who never showed up, the drawings no one wanted to see – and it all ties in. I think back on myself, too, only a couple of days ago, blocking my ears against the unwelcome news Nico wanted to tell me, and I think, if I did that, who am no relation and completely unconnected . . .

The Trombettas of this world deserve admiration, they really do. There she is, a young woman of not even thirty, I would say – shy, dainty, elegant, from a good middle-class background, the sort of girl who a century ago would have been keeping a scrapbook and penning poems in it about buttercups – and what is she doing? Dedicating all her time and energy to plumbing the murky minds of child molesters.

On her rating they come in two main categories: posh and yob. (Which seems a funny way of classifying but in fact makes a certain amount of sense in a pretty senseless field, and has nothing, incidentally, to do with social status.) The yobs, she says, are usually incestuous, mainly for reasons of convenience, and are often victims themselves of early abuse. They inflict violence, strange though it sounds, in order to recover some shred of self-esteem, recoup some vestige of forfeited power. IQs in this group are generally low. Gender selection is not much of an issue: in the main they prefer females, the younger the better, but have a *faute de mieux* attitude towards boys as well. Their sexual relations with adults are often, surfacewise, satisfactory and normal. Rationalising is not much indulged in by them either: they are brutal themselves and in this spirit brutalise others. Do as you have been done by. On the deep psychological plane their erotic objects, so T says, remain just that: objects. (Poor little tiddlers.)

Posh molesters are quite another story. In their case the erotic object is in fact an image of themselves when they were young, hence the erotic object is also an object of unbounded 'Love', in one of the meanings of this versatile word. It follows too that they are prevalently homosexual (although some can apparently function off and on with women as well, provided the women are not too flowery or voluptuous). The drive behind the appetite is, as with the yobs, the rebuilding of shattered vanity, but whereas the yobs, so to speak, are still at the basement stage and happy to remain there, the posh molesters have built a huge edifice already and are busy adding towers and spires and follies. In this sense, says T, they are harder for us to understand and much, much harder to forgive. The typical example is clever, well educated, extremely, extremely sly, and utterly unrepentant. His method of aggression will be spider-slow and will contain a lot of seduction and gentleness and backtracking before violence comes on the scene. And when it does appear, violence too will often wear a mask. Even in communing with the self: the posh paedo is in fact sustained in his wrongdoing by an elaborate safety net of justifications. It is modern-day society that is at fault, not he. In classical Greece the relationship between young boy and elder lover, bla, bla, bla . . . Plato and the caring mentor, Thebes and military male bonding, Templars and Hitler-jugend and the same, Freud and infant sexuality – big *minestrone* of spurious arguments that prove nothing, except that the posh p is brilliant at squaring his conscience.

Trombetta says she has spoken to men in prison who swear blue murder that all they were doing was acting as a kind of godfather to the children involved, helping them enter the harsh adult sexual world in the gentlest possible way. Benefactors. Blooming guardian angels. Others plead an even more radical type of innocence, insisting that their relationships to children have an Arcadian, before-the-fall character, which the children understand perfectly well, being children, and which they themselves understand, being Peter Pans in this respect, but which the dirty-thinking and corrupt adults of society at large misconstrue.

Swallow that if you can. And then come back to me with your own reflections on the matter, because

From: salvia@libero.it
To: sparks@bookhound.com
Subject: to asthma attacks
Date: Sun, Mar 5, 2000, 9.16 p.m.

Si. No, everything's fine. Ish. I didn't sign off last time because I suddenly saw Mitzi's ears swivelling, the way they do when she's attentive, and her tail beginning to beat a welcome tattoo on the tiles, and I realised just in time that Ferdinando had come back without warning. (An olive branch in his beak, or a gauntlet to throw at me? Difficult to tell till he'd crossed the threshold. What would your guess be?) It's stupid of me probably, but he's been so inquisitive recently about what I'm writing that I didn't want him to find me at the computer at all. Particularly not writing an e-mail, and particularly not to you.

So I just shoved it off the way it was. I *think* I acted fast enough. Hope so anyway: whether it's quarrelling or making up quarrels afterwards, our relationship when we're together seems to have slid into a rather airless, claustrophobic groove, and this flusters me slightly, although I know it has a positive side as well and I just have to accept it. I used to have asthma attacks as a child, before I grew out of them, and it's a bit like that: I feel the weight of Ferdinando's attention on me, and in a way that is difficult to describe (because it's my mind I'm talking about, not my lungs or my bronchi) I find it difficult to breathe.

Computers won't be hurried though, and mine took its usual time and made its little farewell beep noise just as he came through the door. However I'm pretty sure he took no note of it. It was a fairly fraught meeting, after so long a silence on both sides: one of those in-the-balance ones that could go one way or could go another – all depending on the first move and who makes it. Like Mitzi's, I think I just saw his head swivel a tiny bit towards the desk and then back to me again, and then he suddenly did something amazing that took my mind off everything else: he went down on his knees on the hard-tiled floor and literally prostrated himself at my feet, trembling all over. Forgive, forgive. Never to abandon him. To stay by him in this terrible phase of his life, as he feels himself getting older and older and uglier and balder and losing all his powers of attraction. To understand, support, commiserate. Yes, there has been someone else, but it was vanity, weakness, it's all over now. It's me he needs, his strong little English anchor who stays firm whatever, without me he is lost. These last few days he's been through hell. He spent his birthday alone in a museum, staring at a Piero della Francesca. He doesn't even know which one: it was only the eyes he saw: two tilted little mirrors of trust and candour that reminded him of mine.

Oh Si, I caved in like the marshmallow that I am. It's the past, the things we've shared, this weight of accumulated experience that drags me to him like the force of gravity itself. And yet it's something more as well. As I bent down to him I had like a lightning vision of our two selves and whatever it is that unites us, as if we were just bones, or a diagram, stripped of all the flesh, all the inessentials: I saw us, these two things – beings, entities, whatever you like to call them – and linking them, or us, I saw this bare, wiry knot, frayed but holding fast, and I knew in that instant there would be no loosening of it ever, whether I wanted it or not.

Bon, that is a personal variant on Getting Back to Basics, but it was very instructive and, as I say, in its stifling way strangely reassuring. Even a prison becomes home if you know you can't leave it, and this marriage is a bit of both to me: home and prison. Perhaps that is true of all lifelong relationships? What says my wise young philosopher friend?

Did we . . .? Oh no, nothing like that, not yet at any rate. The barrier remains, but we have found a Pyramus and Thisbe method of reaching each other through it. We hauled things out into the open at long last, and he admits to having problems (and to their being exclusively *his* problems: they cropped up apparently with the other person as well, and I believe this, because it's not the sort of thing a man like him would willingly confess to); and then we discussed ways of facing them or not facing them as maybe, and I said (and this was true too, because I had just discovered it) that now I knew for certain he still loved me and vice versa, that side of things was not such a big deal any more, we had all the time we needed in front of us, and we drifted off into unconsciousness together, hand in hand, and slept chaste but close, like a medieval lord and lady, with Mitzi *couchant* at the foot of the bed.

And lived happily ever after? No, in the morning we were squabbling again but, as I said, after this glimpse of the basic solidity of our bond, minor divergences have lost their kick. I found myself, after having been all forgiving and superior and not wanting to know, suddenly horribly curious and jealous of this creature he's been seeing, and to my extreme annoyance he wouldn't say a word. Only her name, her Christian name: Elisa, and the fact that she's a student at the university and keen on – yeah, you bet, baroque painting and architecture, and has been helping him in his research. Yuk. As a foil to my questions he turned the tables on me and started being jealous himself, or pretending to be: of my writing, of my time, of my interests, even of my friendship with Nico. Who he hates: it's not that he disapproves of gays because they're gay, but, when in Capri anyway, he has strange little corners of propriety where sex of any kind is concerned. People will talk, he says, if I go around all the time with a man who's not my husband. Doesn't matter whether he's straight or gay or what he is: they will talk, and talk filth, and some of the filth will rub off on him, and on the Acquaviva family.

I.e. on the old witch and the layabout, because that's more or less all that's left of the Acquaviva family. Perhaps I should have said this straight out, but the night's forgiving mood was still on me, and I didn't. In fact, to be scrupulously honest, I think I was rather flattered to find him jealous of me, as well as me of him. It was a pride soother.

However, if you're putting me down as an out-and-out wimp, pause a little over the following data:

1) Despite F's pleas to return with him to Naples this afternoon when he left, I AM STILL HERE.
2) Despite his rather ambivalent attitude to my writing I am still determined to write something. Eventually. When I've decided what.

3) Despite his quite *un*ambivalent attitude to Nico I am going to go on seeing him whenever and as much as I like, especially as I may be losing him soon. And

4) Despite the fact that if I told F about it he'd probably throw another of his mad fits, I have promised myself not to be such a coward over this Tonino thing and listen to whatever it is Nico wants to tell me. I started him off, after all: I reckon it's my duty, if not to go on seconding him and playing Watson, at least to lend him a shred of moral support.

Christ, what a tome. Does anyone in the office ever object to your receiving all this personal material? Or do you keep our correspondence a bit under your hat like I do? All this paedo stuff you've sent me from the Internet – that wouldn't do much good to your reputation in the workplace if anyone found out about it, would it now? Or at home, for that matter. Hope I don't end up ruining your good name.

Yes, it *is* helpful. Many thanks. If only because it shows the research field is in such a mess that Trombetta's theories look to be as good as any others, if not better. Trouble is, in all these various forums and websites you only get to hear the voice of the poshies, but I suppose that's unavoidable – the other sort are unlikely to be computer-articulate. (Except, wait, did you notice the spelling of the man who said, I am borne like this?) Anyway, as regards the poshies, the material seems to bear out everything Trombetta said, all along the line. And this is reassuring because, I didn't get around to this in my last message, but in fact the little *Dottoressa* did slightly fudge it at the end of her lecture. There was this woman in the audience, you see, who got up and said, Ah, yes, that's all very well, but in the park the other day there was this man waylaying little children and molesting them, and he definitely didn't fit into either of the categories you've mentioned inasmuch (and here she gave the details, which I don't remember, but they *were* quite conflicting *vis à vis* the twofold scheme) – now what do you say about that? And Trombetta, instead of arguing, just grabbed a piece of chalk and expanded her classification on the spot, saying, Well, I'm glad you brought that up, I would have done so myself in the next lecture: the paedophile you saw, *Signora*, was in fact our *third* type of offender: the Park Paedophile. I didn't include him in our list today so as not to muddle you. We will examine him in detail next week.

This did rock my faith slightly, I will admit (*and* Lewis Carroll, where does he fit in?), but now all your material has firmed it up again. It's all there, all the signs she said to look for – the psychological fudgery, the pathetic, gossamer excuses; the vanity, the selfishness; the unlimited pity and indulgence the paedos concede to themselves, and the callous unconcern they show towards their victims. 'Never did any kid any harm, to my knowledge.' 'Kids like a bit of rough-and-tumble.' 'Seemed to be enjoying it, didn't realise.' Did you notice how many of the interviews contain bracketed asides (weeps), (breaks down), (sobs), (sighs) and did you notice how it was always in connection with the speaker's own woes, never anything to do with the children's? And did you notice too how the words 'fun' and 'innocence' and 'tenderness' crop up again and again – in a context that makes you wonder if you could have possibly read right? No wonder the phenomenon – though if you think carefully it is a natural one like all others and only needs proper understanding – no wonder it is so sick-making for us, so creepy.

One more quick remark before I close (bet you're the one who's sighing now): another thing that struck me, and wonder if it did you too, is how unbearably prudish most of them are about sex. How DARE they be, the hypocrites. Lots of love, and glad you got the choccies, L.

PS What I said about Ferdinando hating Nico may have been a bit unfair. He doesn't like him, but he was very sensitive towards him once. On the wall outside the villa here someone had sprayed in huge letters A MORTE I RECCHIONI (meaning Death to People with Big Ears, meaning queers – work out that entomology if you can, you spider-lover), and before Nico or his boyfriend could see it and get upset by it, Ferdinando had Carmine scrape it off and re-stucco the wall and repaint. An action like that makes up for a lot of minor narky remarks, wouldn't you agree?

From: salvia@libero.it
To: sparks@bookhound.com
Subject: of biography starts coming to life at last
Date: Wed, Mar 8, 2000, 10.15 a.m.

You are a wizard, Mr Parks. Simon Magus. The ferret is *brilliant*. It ferreted out Fersen straightaway – pages of stuff. Did you visit the site yourself? If so, did you read about how cagy the French Archives were about releasing the names of the boys involved in Fersen's first scandal: the blow-jobs in the bathroom? And this in *1988*, if you please, a mere twelve years ago, eighty-five years after the jobs were blown. Some of those little boys must have grown into quite important old codgers, no, to be able to fix that one?

And did you read the description of one of the tableaux vivants Fersen staged on that occasion: '*An adolescent, stark naked, lying on a white bearskin, his body covered with golden gauze, his forehead crowned with roses and his arms resting on a skull of polished ivory.*' Wonder who that was? Probably Mitterrand or somebody. (Thought skulls were made of bone, though, didn't you?)

And did you see the 'glorification' of boyfriend Nino, wrapped up in a flowered bedspread, with a crown on his pretty noddle? And did you click on the name and find his nude portrait, *sans cheval*?

So busy and *allumée* by all this wealth of material, I must cut short and go straight to work before inspiration fades. Yr grateful literary pal Lola.

PS You ask what Nico had to say that was so important. I didn't tell you because I don't know, he's away for a few days, flat-hunting in Milan, and wouldn't say anything over the telephone when I asked him. Means nothing, he loves to dramatise.

PPS No, I've never locked my mailbox to date – the pass-word is registered or automatic or whatever – and I don't think it's a good idea to start now. If F does by any chance browse a bit now and then, the lock would only strengthen his suspicions, and if he doesn't it's not needed anyway. Much better I just scrap any letters in which I write any-thing uncomplimentary about him and leave it at that. Or maybe – better still – have a big tidy-up and scrap the lot. Do I keep yours? One or two – the ones I like re-reading – but most I erase after I've answered them. And you? What do you do with mine?

PPPS Your paedo musings were a bit above my head. I think I just see what you mean about our condemnation of paedophilia being society's last shared moral certainty, and vital to us on that account, but I fail to grasp the connection with music. Music seems to me one of the few things that's *right* with the world. Sorry to be so thick, L.

From: salvia@libero.it
To: sparks@bookhound.com
Subject: of biography goes down the plughole
Date: Thu, Mar 9, 2000, 3.36 p.m.

From the introduction to your Internet article (which yesterday I'd only skimmed): **COMPLETE FERSEN ARCHIVES ARE TO BE MADE PUBLIC IN YEAR 2003.**

Splosh. Cold shower on all my enthusiasms. Never mine day. And not your fault either, Si, for God's sake don't think that. In fact I'm dead relieved I got the information in time, before I'd gone any further. Think if I'd done nearly all the book – I would have torn my hair out.

Probably a good thing anyway. Now I've read the article properly and combed (hair, comb, blast) through the notes and the bibliography, I realise the task was way beyond me in any case: I haven't got the drive, I haven't got the patience, I haven't got the scholarship or the organising ability. Doubt I've got the sensibility either: the author of the Internet piece seems to view Fersen as a much more serious and tragic figure than I had ever envisaged. I just think he's weak and flabby and faintly ludicrous; I wouldn't be able to give him the treatment he (perhaps) deserves. Plus which, Trombetta and Tonino combined have robbed me of whatever ill-formed fascination I may have felt towards the figure of the paedophile in general, and the posh paedo in particular (which Fersen very definitely was – they don't come much posher.) Vanity, self-indulgence and the capacity to ride roughshod over the needs of others in order to gratify your own – these simply aren't very fascinating qualities full stop.

Oh dear, what now? I suppose I'll just have to gather my things together and traipse back to Naples and Ferdinando and my wifely duties – such as they are. Think I'll wait till after Easter, though, then we'll see. Who knows, perhaps in the meantime I'll manage to think up another pretext for staying put: I seem to be rather a dab hand at pretexts.

The photo of the ascent is *fantastic*, but I begin to understand your turnover of girlfriends a bit now. You can't expect someone to take to that sort of thing on a 'getting to know the ropes' basis, when the ropes dangle over a drop that high. You must either pick another fanatic or resign yourself to weekends of solitude while your current flame stays home on firm ground and washes her underwear.

I'm a fine one to talk, but that is my advice. I wouldn't make her sit through the film Π either – the video shop here got it specially in for me, but I must confess all those creepy-crawlies got the better of me. But then as you know enology leaves me cold. Fond love from (temporarily at any rate) Loose-end Lola.

From: salvia@libero.it
To: sparks@bookhound.com
Subject: of INQUIRY comes OUT of plughole and
           wafts around like an evil genie
Date: Thu, Mar 9, 2000, 11.19 p.m.

Simon, Got to tell you this before I go to bed. Can't sleep anyway, it's set my mind racing in the one direction I don't want it to, and I shall probably have to play computer patience for hours before I can get it to calm down again. Nico is back, and guess what it was he wanted to tell me? The rumour, you remember, the one I refused to listen to and that he wouldn't say over the phone? Well, as I said, it's only a rumour and as such could be just a malicious invention, but it has a loathsome ring of truth about it that comes from the fact that it is so detailed, and in a way so absurd it kind of overtakes invention. See if you don't agree. The fount is dubious: someone who knows someone who knows someone, sort of thing, who works in the morgue. Or used to, or . . . I don't know, there's no checking anything, and nothing really to check. It's just that they have this joke there apparently – the pathologists or whoever – regarding homosexuals and how to spot them. They call it the 'flour test', the reason being that ages ago there was this old ex-army doctor who used to swear that when he was on the officers' selection board he used to make the candidates sit naked on a tub of flour, and then take readings of the imprints to see whether or not they had ever had anal intercourse. It's stupid and revolting, I know, and the test can never really have existed, but that's not the point. The point is that the term stuck, in joke form, and was being bandied about in connection with Tonino after the post-mortem: that he wouldn't have passed the flour test.

Meaning . . . Well, that's pretty clear, isn't it. I don't think I need say any more. But oh God, it upsets me so. True or false, I can hardly bear to think about it. For Nico to have picked it up, *someone* must have said it, in some context, at some point, and I know it's illogical, but I find this thought – the thought of Tonino becoming the subject of a casual, throwaway, smutty remark – almost worse than the thought of him being molested. (Which I'm sure now that he was, I'm *sure*, I'm *SURE*.) The molester, after all, must have had some personal interest in him, no matter how sick, how warped; the gossip spreaders, no: he's nothing to them and never was, just a name for them to snigger over. Wouldn't have passed the flour test. Fancy, only ten, and wouldn't have passed the flour test. I can see them, I can hear them at it, and something inside me shrieks out in anguish – that the world can be so wrong, so full of gratuitous evil.

Sorry, Si. Sorry. It's late, and I'm sitting here with full ashtray and fast emptying bottle of Rosso Solano, getting very maudlin. (But you will see that yourself from the sending time, seeing that that's what your computer shows. Mine is set to time of receipt, and I'm stuck with it because I don't know how to change it.) Nico has already moved on inside his head, the way people do when they are shortly to move houses as well, and his interest has kind of lost its edge. He agrees something needs doing, but all he can advise is that I get a private detective on the job now: find out the exact spot where Tonino fell, suss out the ground, look for footprints, cigarette butts, bits of torn clothing, whatever, and then take the findings to the police in the hope they'll reopen the case. Fat lot of good. I reckon, what with the time that has passed and the pathetically slender evidence we have so far managed to collect, it's all useless: I'm an outsider, a foreigner, I've got no claim; unless I call in Ferdinando or Matilde to back me I've got no real clout; probably, apart from this slightly hysterical sympathy I've worked up for someone I never knew but who touches me in some strange way, I've got no reasons either, not strong enough at any rate to convince other people with. And anyway Nico's off in a couple of days, and by next week will have forgotten all about it, so I'm all on my own again. Could ring Augusta, I suppose, but I don't think it's right to bother her any further, do you? Oh, why did I ever start probing into this affair? Why did I ever let myself start thinking about it? Why did I ever stop in front of that grave and see that photograph and let it print itself on my memory?

Why did I ever start thinking about paedophiles too? Oh, I know, it's easy for me to trot out the routine answer I've given so far, that I found them interesting/fascinating/alien/disturbing, couldn't get my mind round them, thought they were good topical material to write about, etc., etc., but that's only part of me speaking. My rational part, my daylight part. Another part, deep inside somewhere, knows there's more to it than that. Perhaps – oh Christ, perhaps this huge tenderness I feel towards children – the longing I have for them – the privation I feel in not being able to bear a child myself – perhaps . . .

No, it's not possible. I hurt a puppy once. Not badly, I just scared it, used it as a railway bridge to run a toy train under. I was being bullied at school, and I came back and grabbed the poor little thing and made it stand still while I ran the train under its legs, and this gave me a sense of power – sweet and flooding like an orgasm. It was about the only violent thing I think I've ever done. No Gilles de Retz, but it shows there's a cruel streak inside me, no? And perhaps it's this cruel streak that for some reason is stirred by the idea . . .

No, it's not possible. But a few nights ago I had this dream, Si: that I was in a house with a long, long corridor and lots of doors leading off it, and some force was propelling me down the corridor towards a little red room that I knew was there but didn't want to enter, because it contained something dreadful that I didn't want to see. And I dug in my heels and tried to resist, but the force got stronger and stronger, and down the corridor I went willy-nilly, clutching on to the other doors to try and stop myself but each time being torn away, until there was only one door left, and it was ajar and I could already see the hangings, and they were deep, deep red . . .

And then mercifully I woke up. But I'm no psychological innocent, or not entirely, I know dreams like this mean something, and in my case I think the meaning is not very hard to decipher: there's some secret inside me – a place perhaps, perhaps a piece of knowledge – that I can't visit, can't touch on, can't admit to being there. Maybe I'm only saying this because I'm pissed, and maybe it's only some home-made ghost from childhood, like a fantasy of my father raping me or something (and maybe, if I think that, I've simply been reading too much Freud), but the possibility scares me sick. In horror movies the threat usually comes from outside – sneaks through a window, lurks behind a door – but what if it's *inside*? Isn't that worse? Oh yes, it is, it's far, far worse.

Thank God it's nearly Friday, and thank God Ferdinando is coming nice and early tomorrow and that all is smooth between us again. This time I don't care how cross he gets, I'm going to tell him everything, shovel it all on to his broad shoulders and let him help me carry the weight. I think he'll do it willingly – it'll make him feel less guilty about his recent escapade. Writing this to you is a huge comfort, Si, and receiving your answers even more so, but just now I need someone *with me, here, physically, to talk to, face to face*. I'm sure you know what I mean.

Brilliant idea: why don't you come for Easter? Oh, why DON'T you? Then you could assuage your curiosity about Matilde. I warn you however that she might prove a divisive factor between us, because with new acquaintances, particularly if they are male, she pulls out her wand and transforms herself into the most enchanting being imaginable. Eighty-one and wicked as sin, but whatever limelight there is, it is hers and she mops it up and glows in it. You would love her, and think me mean-spirited and possibly jealous for not doing likewise, and she would follow all this with her yellow snaky eyes, and relish it, and swiftly, when you were not looking, out would flick her forked tongue and she would pass it over her lips in satisfaction and give a triumphant grin in my direction.

Or perhaps she wouldn't even bother: I'm no fun for her,

it's like Tyson up against a midget. What's so terrible about her? What does she do to merit this invective? That's where her genius lies: she *is* terrible, I swear she is, but you can't really say why or in what way. All you can do is point to the mangled corpses in her wake – her shadowy, ineffectual husband, dead at forty, her bedridden dropout younger son, the benumbed shopkeepers, the sacked retainers, her pathetic, silent sister who sits all day embroidering vestments with sacred hearts and fishes and IHS (Ferdinando is to my knowledge the only close contact to have escaped intact) – and hope for their own sakes people will twig there is some connection.

Must quit now, all this baccy is giving me a sore throat. But think it over, will you? Would it offend you if I offered to stand you the air fare? I spend so much money on things I don't really like that it would be a change and a pleasure. Good for your Italian too. *Pensaci*, big hug, Lola.

From: salvia@libero.it
To: sparks@bookhound.com
Subject: our correspondence
Date: Fri, Mar 10, 2000, 11.21 a.m.

One brief question, Simon. I would be grateful if you could answer immediately. Do you keep a record of our correspondence? No particular reason, I just need to know. All is well. Love, Lola.

From: salvia@libero.it
To: sparks@bookhound.com
Subject: also thank god to moments of total
           contentment
Date: Mon, Mar 13, 2000, 10.23 a.m.

Blissful morning and blissfully happy. Can't think why I've been so whingey lately: must be the solitude. Maybe you're right and I'm not really cut out for the ivory tower habitat at all. As from today, however, things are going to change. In the first place a nice young American couple have just rented the villa next door to me on the other side, so when Nico leaves, as he does this Wed that ever is, poor Nico, then I won't feel so abandoned. Names are Toby and Ben, and Toby for a change is a she. (And no, silly, Ben isn't.) And in the second place Ferdinando has been angelic and, far from being cross or mad, has listened to all my rantings *con amore* and promised to help me in any and every way he possibly can. He's going to work less, and be here much much more (if I want him to be, that is, he's very sweet and humble about deferring to my wishes), and over Easter, if it's still upsetting me, he's going to take a long hol, and dedicate time and thought to the Tonino ghost and how to lay it. He's still totally agin my theory, thinks I'm dotty and badly affected by what he calls the Miss Marple syndrome, but he says that doesn't matter: what he wants is to see me reassured and happy, and to this end he will do anything, pester the Mayor, the Prefect, the Commander of the *Carabinieri*, anybody who can help put my mind at rest. If it'd do any good, he'll even take Nico's place, and chase round the island with me in tandem, hunting for imaginary paedophiles. (My interest in the subject seems to amuse him now, instead of angering him, and he spent all weekend glued to the computer, surfing the net for naughty sites. I couldn't get a look-in.)

My basic problem, he thinks, and he's probably right about this, is still the old childlessness thing, and he's promised that when he's here we'll talk about that too. Properly. Seriously. He's anti adoption – I told you he was – but he says there are other things we can look into. Like fostering, for instance, or having some child from an urban area to stay during the summer, or else I could maybe get a teaching job of some sort, or . . .

Don't know if any of these options would work either, if translated into reality, but that isn't the point. It's the concern that counts. What better proof of love can people give you really, apart from that? None: if you care for someone then you think about them and worry over them and try to help them, it is as straightforward as that. Sex simply doesn't come into the picture. (And speaking of pictures, F has begun painting my portrait in oils – he's dead choosy about the subjects he paints, so I take that as a good sign too.)

Ergo, he loves me. And if this conclusion is important to me – and it *is*, it *is* – then *ergo*, I love him too. So it looks like you were right, Si, all along: I love him and am jealous of him, and all this show of independence – my coming here on my own, pretending to research things, pretending to write – was just that: an empty show, a bluff, a whistling in the dark. If my letters slack off a bit now it will only be on account of the fact that I am well and busy. And *cherished*. Picture me bustling around doing boring wifely things, like planting geraniums and choosing new chair covers and having the terrace furniture revarnished, and all the while happier inside than I have been for ages, because at last I have got my priorities sorted out. All well with my trivial little cosy little bourgeois world.

Keep writing, though, if you can. Let me know about the graphic designer and how things are working out on that front. It's about time your luck turned too in the sentimental stakes. Of the three of us, that would leave only Nico still broken-hearted. Poor Nico, his going will leave such a hole in my life. The Yanks are charming, but they need everything spelling out to them – all my silly banter falls at their feet unfielded and lies there flat as wetted waffles. Last night I lent them the video of *Topsy Turvy*, and they returned it this morning with the criticism that they found it racist. On what account? Principally on account of the names: a real orientalist would have taken more trouble to make them sound convincing. They're here till June, but I don't somehow think we're going to become best buddies in that interval. Nmd.

A big electronic hug, and let me know about Easter, I really mean it. L.

From: salvia@libero.it
To: sparks@bookhound.com
Subject: to mysterious huffs
Date: Tue, Mar 14, 2000, 3.37 p.m.

Simon Stylites, now all of a sudden, on your high column. What a funny stiff businessy letter. What have I said to offend you? Is it the ticket, or what? Anyway, my number is 081837921 + prefix for Italy 0039 (not sure whether the nought before the eight is knocked off or not, try both), so perhaps you will explain when you ring. Unaltered love, L.

From: salvia@libero.it
To: sparks@bookhound.com
Subject: to unwelcome scrutiny
Date: Wed, Mar 15, 2000, 7.44 p.m.

Si, all this afternoon, practically from the moment I put the phone down, I thought. I mooched around the Certosa, that I always find a good place for thinking in, and thought and thought and thought, and I've come to the conclusion that it *must* be jealousy. After all, what other reason could there possibly be? Not *physical* jealousy exactly – I grant you that point – but possessiveness, unwillingness to share me, even mentally, even only a certain part of me, with some other person. Specially a man. Maybe, who knows, a pinch of Italian inferiority complex mixed in too: there they go, scribble scribble, natter natter, in their own wretched language (that I can never *quite* master in spite of the Berlitz), and me, the Wop, cut out of the game, left on the sidelines.

Apart from this I can conceive of no other explanation. So don't WORRY about me, don't fret. It is because he *loves* me in his strange dog-in-the-manger way, because he needs me, because he's terrified that in any sphere whatsoever I may be slipping away from him. He was the same about Nico, remember? Same about Althea, to some extent.

119

He's been the same about my writing too. Think back on what I told you about Fersen, how funny and resentful he was about my choosing that particular subject – as if I was poaching on his domain. Well, it wasn't Fersen he was standing guard over, it was me. Don't you see it now? I do, I see it all as clear as daylight, and, as I said before, part of me feels smothered and another part feels protected, almost cosseted. He cares about me, Si, he cares desperately, and aside from the minor irritation I may feel now and again at the way he shows it, this is basically all that matters. (He's jealous of all my outside interests, now I come to think of it: threw another mad fit, for example, when he first found me reading the paedo book. Went all bulgy-eyed, and said what did I want to read that muck for? Called it *zozzimma*, which is stronger than muck in Neapolitan. Made me feel guilty and bewildered at the same time, rather like I did aged eight when, having just been told in Catechism class that the word meant a young girl, I went and informed my father proudly I was a virgin, sparking off an unforeseen reaction.)

It's a violation of privacy. Yup, OK, but I spied on him too, didn't I, so on that front we're quits. He's written to you, pretending to be me, to see if you are keeping my letters, but I have already broken into his voice mail to see what *he* was up to. Love fifteen, fifteen all. (And it *is* love, Si, you must believe me about this: it is love – on both sides. You don't know him, I wish you did, but he's *not in the least bit* twisted or cruel or sinister or any of the things you fear. He's not even all that selfish really – not compared to other Italian males his age. OK, Matilde spoilt him a bit because he was the eldest son and her favourite, but she sat on him hard as well. And still does –

imposes on him no end: buy me this, fetch me that, take me there. And he buys and fetches and takes like a little lamb. Last summer when she came here he had to escort her up to the villa on one of those electric buggy arrangements together with Ethiopian maid, slavering pug, huge mountain of luggage, two crates of potted plants and twenty-four packets of special pugfood which can't be obtained locally. And he who hates inelegant travel or catching the public eye in any way. So you see?)

How clever you were, though, to spot the message. I knew those silly headings of mine would come in useful some day, but even so, I think it was pretty, pretty sharp of you to cotton on so fast. *Bravo, Simone*. And cleverer still to handle it the way you did. After such a laid-back answer to the negative, F should be able to unwind.

I've thought about the practical side of things too, and, as you can see from this message, I've decided we can go on using this channel – why the hell shouldn't we, it's not as if we had anything to hide – but from now onward WITH CERTAIN ANTI-F PRECAUTIONS:

* Neither of us will ever link messages. We never have done in the past, that I remember, but we'll be double careful not to do so in the future. OK?
* What you do your end is your affair – nobody presumably peers into your mailbox, or do they? – but I will keep on record none of my proper messages to you any more, nor yours to me. They will go straight into my virtual trash bin, and the bin will be emptied, and the back-up of the bin, if there is one (is there? If so how do I find it?), will be emptied too.

* To ward off any further suspicion on F's part we will both, now and again, you *and* me, send each other a friendly business-cum-chat letter on the lines of the one you sent in answer to his: Mitzi, weather, films, books, etc., dead dull, dead pedestrian, just the odd little piece of tripe to make it convincing, and ALL of these letters I will deliberately keep. In fact I will knock off one now, the moment I am through with this.
* The 'Subject' habit proved useful and I will continue it – but not in the fake letters, only in the proper ones. No silly flat puns or whatever on the heading, and you can bet your beret the writer is not me.

Anything else? No, I think that's all for the time being. When you write properly, write mid-week, mid-morning, so that I am the one who opens the post bag. And even when you write properly, NEVER put anything that could be misconstrude. (And *à propos* miscontrude, a deliberate error like that could act as another private signal, no? Or is that a bad idea? Yeah, I'm afraid it's rotten.) Don't ring again unless you have to, as F will be here almost on commuter basis as from next week, or so he says. But, again, if you do ring, keep to the above times.

Nearly bathing weather. Good: beach life will console me for the loss of N who left this morning – v sad. Love, L.

PS I renew the invite for Easter. If F has Matilde as his guest, I don't see why I can't have you as mine. And besides, the more open and above board our friendship is, the less he will feel threatened by it, and the happier everyone will be.

* * *

PPS If Ferdinando should ever read this letter, what *WOULD* he think we were up to?! Just shows how counterproductive jealousy is. He is literally chasing us into each other's mailbox.

From: salvia@libero.it
To: sparks@bookhound.com
Subject: Capri Witches
Date: Wed, Mar 15, 2000, 7.44 p.m.

Dear Simon, today is (are?) the ides of March and it strikes me it is quite a while since I enquired about the books on order. Any luck?

In your last letter you asked how work is progressing. Alas, it isn't. Mainly because, due to this business of the archives, I have had to revert to my first – or was it second or third? – idea, namely the Capri Witch Project, and to scrap Fersen altogether, although I still want the books about him as a present for Ferdinando. Who is my husband, in case you don't remember.

Apropos of witch (this is a joke, not a spelling mistake), if you have anything interesting on hand on that subject as well – cheapish, and for the general reader, not for scholars – please let me know, as I would gladly consider buying.

Hope you are well and happy and that your new girl-friend is less picky than the last. Love, L.

From: salvia@libero.it
To: sparks@bookhound.com
Subject: of witches
Date: Wed, Mar 15, 2000, 8.12 p.m.

The subject of witches, just in case your unscrupulous trade tricks get the better of you, is a **red herring**, like the rest of the letter, and I haven't the slightest intention of writing so much as a line about them nor ever did have. It was just a *façon de parler*. My **true request** is for you to send me just one book about them – it would make our phoney letter exchange look more convincing – but I beg of you to make it *not more than one*, and a slim one at that. In reality anything to do with witches and witchcraft bores me nutty. *Et toi, Brute?* Goodnight, sweet pen pal, L.

From: salvia@libero.it
To: sparks@bookhound.com
Subject: me to no more sermons, please
Date: Fri, Mar 17, 2000, 11.09 a.m.

I don't think I follow you, Mr Nosy Parks, nor you me. You ticked me off before for spying on F, when I had at least some reason to do so, and now, when there is NO REASON any more, you urge me to do so.

And in what dramatic Brazilian soap-opera terms. Why? What's got into you? What on earth can you possibly be afraid of on my account? That he is still two-timing me?

Oh relax, Si. If that possibility doesn't worry me, it shouldn't worry you, should it now? And it *doesn't* worry me. I repeat: things are so much better now, F is dear, attentive, affectionate again; the air is clearer between us, we've both calmed down a lot. Believe me, *tutto va bene*. Marriages *do* go through difficult patches, and it was your misfortune to come across me when mine was navigating just such a one, so that you had to bear the proxy weight of all my whinges, all my groans.

And vice versa it was my *immense* good luck to come across you. I shall always be amazed and grateful for all the time and patience and sympathy that you dedicated to me in those dark winter days when sometimes, literally, my computer screen with your message on it was the only bright spot. But don't spoil the memory now by these weird hints and innuendoes. If there's any precise thing that's bugging you, for God's sake come clean and say it. If not, then be your dear co-operative self and belt up. I was drunk when I wrote you that stuff about the dream – and anyway that's all it was: a dream, an everyday, everynight, common or garden dream. What about yours, then, and the bicycle dealer? I don't bang on at you to 'dwell on the implications' of that, do I? Although I bet any analyst would have a field day with it.

As a matter of fact I am not so naive as you think, and I HAVE been doing just a tiny bit of intelligence work – just checking, just to make sure. And the only unfamiliar voice I've come across on F's answer service is a man from a shop in Naples, telling him the Play Station game he ordered has arrived. Quite what he wants with a thing like that, I don't know – he hates computer games – but I imagine it's a present for some friend's kid or something. Anyway, nothing to bother about: it's not the sort of thing you give a girlfriend, so in that regard I reckon he's clean as a whistle. (And why are whistles clean, incidentally? Get to work on that one: I far prefer you in your old entomologist guise.)

Lack of phone messages isn't much to go by, you will say: you didn't find any before, did you, and yet . . . woozy, woozy, there he was dating a twenty-year-old. I know, wise guy, but this time it's different. So different that I don't really need any proof of his fidelity any more, negative or otherwise. I am happy about him in my head. Happy about him, happy about me, happy about the relationship. And this is a fact: I am not conning myself, or trying to accustom myself to chains by pretending they are bracelets, or being weak or wimpish or pulling wool over my own eyes or any of the things you accuse me of doing. I am simply OK at last. Settled. Content with my lot and looking forward to the future, *in saecula saeculorum*, Amen.

No hurry, but let me know about Easter. It would be fantastic if you could come, and then you could meet Ferdinando and see for yourself how perfectly nice and ordinary and harmless he is. And he could do the same with you, and we could all be friends together – disappointing Matilde who has a great appetite for DRAMA. Must go now – Mlle Toby has come round, asking could she borrow an adaptor, and I shall have to be neighbourly and go and dig one out. Best love, Lola.

From: salvia@libero.it
To: sparks@bookhound.com
Subject: that dare not write its name
Date: Thu, Mar 23, 2000, 9.07 a.m.

Sorry I haven't written, Si, but I told you to interpret silence as a good sign. Very busy at present getting things into shape for the summer: Capri climate is corrosive of things like paint and canvas. If you had a Rembrandt or whatever it would *not* be the place to keep it. Haven't had much time for brooding either – on anything – and can't say I regret it. Winter, crisis, loneliness, boredom and my stratagems for beating it – all seem aeons away.

Ferdinando is busy too; shuttles back and forth to Naples daily like a city stockbroker, little black case in hand, and in the evening I meet him at the top of the funicular and we have a glass of wine together in the *piazzetta* and then waddle off home in the twilight like the seasoned old couple we are, and before long I shan't be surprised if I start calling him Ferdie and finding that the name fits. I've tried it once or twice in my head: Ferdie, Ferdie. Yeah, it could be he's growing into a nice cosy old Ferdie.

You'll be able to judge for yourself when you come. I'm thrilled to think there's a chance you can make it, but I'm not thrilled at your reason. You must come, if you come, on *positive* grounds: because you want to give your new girlfriend a hol, or yourself a hol, or because you want to see Capri, or meet me, or boggle at Matilde, or go climbing or whatever. Your stated *negative* intent, i.e. to tell me something you cannot bring yourself to say to me over the wires but only face to face, quite honestly I find rather saddening. Since when has our correspondence taken this crippling and self-destructive turn?

Besides, I think I know perfectly well what it is – this subject that dare not write its name. I'm thirty-seven after all, and I haven't lived on an island all my life, and even if I had, *this* island, tiny though it is, would have enlightened me. You think he may be gay, that's what it is: you think Ferdinando may be gay, and that it has never crossed my mind to suspect it.

Oh come off it, Si. Of course I've suspected it. To some extent still do. But what the hell. If I've never spoken to you about it in my letters it wasn't that I was embarrassed or reluctant or too cowardly to face up to that possibility, it was just quite honestly that it didn't – doesn't – seem to matter. No big issue with me either way. I mind about the sex, yes, but because it's a vehicle of tenderness. The Ferrari, maybe, of vehicles of tenderness. However, if, as it's doing now, tenderness uses another means of travel, what do I care whether it rides in a Fiat or a bus or a taxi or even a bike, just as long as it reaches me in the end. If Ferdinando is happy then he is tender towards me, and if he is tender then I am happy and find it easier to make him happy and so forth, and we get carried upwards in a spiral, like a booming economy. Vice versa, when he's unhappy we sometimes get locked, as we did this winter, in a downward spiral, and then everything goes slumpwards.

134

If he is . . . no, not if he *is* homosexual, that would imply he'd already sorted this side of himself out, but if he has let's say homosexual *tendencies*, then whether he follows them or smothers them – and at his age he must surely have done either one or the other or both – they obviously don't make him happy. In a certain and very important sense, therefore, his sexual orientation is something that stands outside our marriage, doesn't touch it. The knot I described to you is unaffected by it and comes under no strain on that account.

I hope this makes sense to you, but if it doesn't . . . nmd. Essential thing is that it should make sense to me. Fond love (and cool it a bit in your bookish imagination – I can't think what you mean by the reference to Browning's 'My Last Duchess' or see anything ominous in the portrait F is painting of me. I have no copy of Browning's poems here and don't like them anyway), L.

PS And now comes a falsie for my files. Fraid it'll be a limp one, I seem to have run out of fuel.

From: salvia@libero.it
To: sparks@bookhound.com
Subject: Mediterranean witches
Date: Thu, Mar 23, 2000, 9.08 a.m.

Dear Simon, witch no. I must be travelling by broomstick, she is taking so long to arrive. The other book you suggest sounds a bit too detailed, and a bit too Nordic also – I have a feeling the phenomenon of witchcraft must have been a whole different ball game this side of the Alps. Could you be an angel and just keep it on ice till I decide?

Weather lousy at pres. Much to Mitzi's relief: she loathes the heat and in her view the longer it postpones its arrival the better. (Only point of divergence in our otherwise synoptic world picture.)

In haste, as the weekend approaches and I have shopping to do. Love, Lola.

From: salvia@libero.it
To: sparks@bookhound.com
Subject: me to no more of this, full stop
Date: Wed, Mar 29, 2000, 4.46 p.m.

Simon. The poem you sent – 'My Last Duchess': either it's a joke or you're serious. If it's a joke it's not very funny; if it's meant seriously it *is* quite funny but it doesn't make me laugh. In both cases, seeing that I am a duchess and have an Italian husband and happen to be sitting for my portrait etc., and have been through rather a bad patch recently in my marital life, I find it in startlingly bad taste.

In my last proper letter I thought I made things clear: this correspondence thrives insofar (and in so long) as we are open with each other. I don't call your present behaviour open, I call it oblique and snide and – yes, why not, downright offensive also. Particularly in Ferdinando's regard.

No really hard feelings, only medium hard, but let's just suspend things between us for a while, shall we? L.

From: salvia@libero.it
To: sparks@bookhound.com
Subject: Re: <no subject>
Date: Tue, Apr 4, 2000, 11.16 p.m.

Simon. Oh Simon oh Simon, something has happened. Oh Si, I'm so sorry I cut you off like that, but you'll know already, the moment you get this, why I did so and why I

From: salvia@libero.it
To: sparks@bookhound.com
Subject: I was discussing earlier when we were interrupted
Date: Wed, Apr 5, 2000, 2:48 a.m.

Si, Quickly, just in case he wakes and I can't finish – FOR GOD'S SAKE DON'T TELEPHONE OR WRITE ANY MORE PROPER LETTERS

Wait for my next message. I'm perfectly OK, but I've found something and I need to talk to you about it. You'll know already I think more or less what it is. You'll forgive me also for my silence and crossness and hedgings of late, of this I'm sure. What a fool I've been. Nmd (but it takes some facing up to, you will admit), L.

From: salvia@libero.it
To: sparks@bookhound.com
Subject: can't think of what to put, but it is me, I
           promise
Date: Thu, Apr 6, 2000, 9.32 a.m.

Si, I've seen him on to the boat for Naples so I know it's safe to sit down and write. I think you know – I'm pretty well sure you know – what it is I have to say to you, but all the same it's difficult and I hardly know where to start. Perhaps I'd better go back to Tuesday.

On Tuesday afternoon, almost evening it must have been because F was due any moment, Toby came round to bring back the adaptor she borrowed, having bought one for herself in the meantime, and we sat on the terrace a bit and chatted, and then when she'd left I went inside to put the adaptor away in the cupboard where we keep all the tools and electric stuff, and that was when I saw it.

It was nothing. It is nothing, no proof, no certainty to build an accusation on – just a cardboard box which once housed one of these electronic Game Boy things, bought in Japan, I reckon, three or four years ago when F was there on business, with the instructions and guarantee still inside. But, Si, the moment I saw it something in my head clicked, and I saw, first, an old picture of him – a glimpse I caught once and must have archived, of him in Naples, walking down a street at dusk in the company of a young boy, fitting his steps to the boy's, skipping almost – and then, cancelling out the old one, a new picture sprang into being – so ugly, so horrifying, it froze me. The Play Station, remember? The call from the toy shop in Naples on his answer service? He buys toys. He buys toys for little boys. He bought them then and he is still buying them now.

The girl – Elisa – does not exist. Or if she does she exists like I do – as a flat foldable object to be toted around and set up and used as a screen. His love-life, if you can call it that, his emotional life, the life of his passions, is played out in quite another dimension – in the moral vortex that the screen so obligingly conceals. He is a paedophile, Simon, that is the raw truth of the matter. My husband is a paedophile. I am married to a paedophile, and, worse, I am tied to and enmeshed with and dependent on and in love with a paedophile.

But then you knew that already, didn't you? And so, probably, did I, and have done for much longer than I care to admit. Only the acknowledgement of the knowledge was lacking. In England I have this little niece – my cousin's daughter – who once said to me: Lola, my brain knows more than I do. I laughed at the time because it sounded funny, but she was right: our brains know more than we do. My brain knows more than I do. Without letting on to the rest of me, or, to be more precise, without the rest of me *allowing* itself to be let on to, my brain has contained this piece of information for months now, maybe even years. Why else did I fix my mind on Fersen in the first place? Why did the villa Lysis fascinate me so? Why did I want those books on paedophilia? Why did I attend that lecture, take those notes?

I knew, Si, that is the other raw truth of the matter. You were right to keep on at me. The dream, the red room – you were right to try and make me enter it. I've been a coward and I've been in bondage, and I've worn shackles and my eyes have been blindfolded, and I've just lain there and endured it. The single bits of knowledge were all there, like the stones of a mosaic; it was just a question of fitting them together and daring to look at the result. The identikit of the paedophile according to Trombetta – why, it could have been his photograph: the vanity, the secrecy, the cunning, the terrible insecurity that afflicts him and that makes him – I don't know how to explain it – sort of hollow at his centre. You knock on his heart and it's empty. You beg audience and hear only the echo of your own voice. And then the ruthlessness that accompanies it all – the way he can spurn me and leave me bleeding, with no comfort, no explanation. His absurd quest for perfection in silly little things, and his fury when I fail to supply it. He could make love to me in the beginning because I looked like a boy myself; the operation spoilt me for him: I had a womb, and the scar betrayed its presence. Or else – I don't know – it put him in mind of a cracked vase or something, or torn material or . . .

Oh Si, what do I do? What do I do now that I've entered the room and seen the horror? Who do I turn to? How do I carry on with my life?

He comes back this evening, and maybe I'm still numb and able to sort of sleepwalk around the way I've been doing since Tuesday. (He doesn't notice my moods much and never has, and this is a relief.) But maybe I'll have flipped, maybe the anguish will be such, I'll be unable to contain it.

WHAT DO I DO FOR GOD'S SAKE? WHAT DO I DO?

And don't answer this, either, I beg of you. Don't ring, don't write. I may ring you myself later this morning, when you've had time to take this in and do some thinking. If not, I'll ring tomorrow lunchtime. I feel I would like to go down to the sea and just plunge in and not come out again, the way Tonino did.

Tonino. That is another room that needs entering, but not now, not now. L.

From: salvia@libero.it
To: sparks@bookhound.com
Subject: needs examining by the cool light of reason
Date: Fri, Apr 7, 2000, 10.47 a.m.

All right, I'll do my best, I'll try to be logical about it – keep my head, weigh the evidence, give him a fair trial. (Funny you should be the one using the brake now. First you push me down the slope, then you complain I'm going too fast.)

Well, there's my mental picture of him and the child, for a start. It's not an imagining, it's a memory. Definitely. I don't remember when it was, that's asking too much, but it must be several years ago now. A rainy evening, autumn or spring. Probably autumn, I think. A street – not in our neighbourhood, somewhere anonymous, central, some-where I don't usually go and am not expecting to see him; a café, a shoeshop, me pausing by the shop window to look at some shoes, and then suddenly seeing him, as I pick my head up, quite a distance away but clearly recog-nisable all the same, in his corduroy jacket with the leather patches on the elbows, just sauntering along the same way I'm going, in the company of a child. A boy. It's a dead ordinary picture, nothing strange about it at all – could have been any child, son of a friend, a *scugnizzo* who's touching him for money, anyone – and it couldn't have struck me as strange at the time, could it, or I'd remember the feeling of strangeness, and I don't. No, the only strange thing is its complete and total disappearance from my memory and then its coming back when it did, with the force that it did. (Which, OK, is begging the question. I know enough about logic to know that. But still.)

Then there's the sex. I've bored you enough about that already, but it's a fact. Objective. Not part of my imaginings. This inability of his to make love to me any more, while at the same time wanting me, needing me desperately, in a way that up till now simply hasn't made sense, and now suddenly does.

Then there's – I don't know if this counts – but there's his caginess about his past. Which, although I've never really admitted this either, neither to myself nor to anyone else, has *always* puzzled me, *always* bothered me, *always* created a kind of barrier between us. (Perhaps I mentioned it to you once. Did I? And did I say how worrying I found it? Well, maybe not – there've been several worries I've kept to myself – but I did.)

Then there's the games – the computer games. Real enough in themselves, but you're right, I don't have any proof what he does with them, except I know he doesn't play with them himself.

And what about tampering with your wife's e-mail to find out if her correspondent keeps her letters? That's factual enough. With the motive behind not jealousy but fear – fear of exposure.

And what about his disapproval of homosexuals? And what about *the writing on the wall*?

Interruption here. Plumber came. (The question of Capri drains and how badly they work sickens me now: I can't help tying it in with my own situation – the façade of my marriage, and the stinking, overflowing cesspit beneath. I wanted worms, did I, well, I've got them by the canful.) I meant to tackle the Tonino question point by point, I've even made notes of it, in a private code – how paranoid can you get? – but I can't write any more now, I'm so scared he may come back. He's not due till this evening but all the same I'm just not relaxed enough to go on sitting here with my nose to the computer and my back to the terrace. I have to keep a check on things.

Assunta is here. I've no idea what old-fashioned looks are, nor do I ever normally use the term, but if I had to describe the way she looks at me, that's the way I'd describe it. Old-fashioned. She's picked up some vibes and knows that something big is happening or about to happen. Mitzi likewise. Thank God I've got her chip organised.

Mitzi's, you fool. Oh Si, I know I don't really know you properly, and that I can't miss you, never having met you, but I do, I miss you *terribly*. Who else can I talk to? I've rung Althea for comfort, and Nico and my mum, but when it came to the crucial bit I funked telling them. The only other person I'm accustomed to run to in times of trouble is F himself . . . Some comfort. (And what if *he* picks up the vibes, eh? They're all over the place, judging from A & M. What if he picks them up? What in shit's name do I do then? I want no confrontation yet, I don't know what to say, I don't know what to think, I don't even know how to go about thinking. My head is like a spin drier, and inside is a white sheet with bloodstains: the ghost of Tonino, tumbling around, waiting for the spinning to stop.) L.

From: salvia@libero.it
To: sparks@bookhound.com
Subject: ing myself to inner scrutiny
Date: Mon, Apr 10, 2000, 11.52 a.m.

You dope, you know perfectly well what I meant by the writing on the wall: I meant the graffito about queers on the wall outside that we thought was meant for Nico and partner, and that F made Carmine whitewash over in a hurry . . . Anyway you know perfectly well what I mean: *He couldn't leave it there, because it was aimed at him.*

And don't for God's sake turn flippant on me, even if your intent is to lighten my heart. I nearly *died* when I saw your message. He's resourceful, you know, and he's alert: it's all I can do to stop my own messages reaching him – body language and the rest – I don't want to have to be on the lookout for yours as well. DON'T WRITE – I say this – shriek this – for the last time. Only straightforward business, and only at longish intervals at that. He keeps a keen eye on the computer, I know he does; he's sensed I'm on to something – he keeps a keen eye on me, on everything. His work hours are all different now – no pattern, he shows up when least I expect it. (And remember, in my business letters I will always begin my message with a word in the lower case – then you know it's me OK but you also know it's not a real letter. Plus which I will use the mistake idea as well, and insert a discreet spelling error: F would never do that in English, he would check and check, he is so vain. God, these precautions, they scare me almost worse than whatever it is they're meant to avoid.)

Just now I know I'm safe. I've bought a little machine thing that I clip on to the phone when he's out, and it shows me the number he's ringing from. He rang a few minutes ago and he's in Naples. Says he won't be back till evening, but I'll leave a margin and take it to mean afternoon. Anyway, whichever, at least I've got time to write properly and tell you what's happening and the way my thoughts are going.

I live, Si, as if I have a huge raw potato in my gullet. Food won't go down, breath won't enter or exit smoothly. I wake in the morning, early, dreadfully early, and it's the first thing I am aware of: this pressure above the sternum, this tightness, this fluttering, beating lump of God knows what. More than a potato, it sometimes feels as if it's alive – a trapped bird or something. Its manifestations are those of panic, but I think its real name is misery.

It's the last deduction I find so difficult to make, the last step. Like mountaineers as they reach the summit, my feet get heavier and heavier, my progress slower and slower, the effort involved greater and greater. Let's see if I can make it today:

* Ferdinando was in Capri when Tonino died. He told me nothing. A child fell to his death – what would it be? Half a kilometre from here, three-quarters at the most, *while* Ferdinando was here, and he told me nothing.

* Nobody told me anything. (And there is no defence mechanism at work, not here at any rate. It's not as if I *was*

154

in fact told, and then, like the woman Trombetta's story, 'forgot' because the knowledge was such that I couldn't take it on board. No, the knowledge would have meant little to me then, beyond the inherent sadness of the fact itself. I might have put 0.2 and 0.2 together to make 0.4, even 1.2 and 1.2 to make 2.4, but further than this I would not have gone. Just over the halfway mark, no further.) So, no, I'm not fudging here: for reasons best known to themselves, and probably for as many different reasons as there were different cases, nobody ever told me anything.

* And yet some people, at some level, must have felt, sensed, suspected there was some connection between me and the death. Their silence is no proof of this, of course, silence is seldom proof of anything, but it's a strong indication. Assunta won't speak. The cashier lady wouldn't speak. The headmistress wouldn't speak. Carmine spat into the flowerbeds. The woman in the cemetery spat on my plait of heather. *Nun saccio* – I know nothing: the classic southern response to any query whose answer may involve or compromise the person interrogated. Prudence first. How many of them were acting on this principle in a general way, out of habit or training? All of them? Or did some of them in fact have a *particular* reason for keeping silent?

I suspect the latter. (Oh fuck these margins – excuse my language. Even in my present state they rile me.) And specifically I suspect Carmine and Assunta. The others, I would think, were acting on hunch or hearsay: those two, no, they knew something. They live in close contact with us, they know something.

Strangely though – or is it perhaps a predictable reaction? – the question of what they knew or know fades to insignificance in my mind at present. What obsesses me is to find out what I KNEW and what I KNOW. Is it shame, Si? What is it that drives me? Is it guilt? And if so, shame at what, and guilt over what?

Do I think that if I'd known earlier, recognised earlier, I could have done something to save Tonino? Do I perhaps think that I *did* know? I CANNOT WORK IT OUT in my head, I CANNOT WORK IT OUT. Abused child meets (accidental? deliberate?) death in the vicinity; my husband is a child abuser; therefore it is my husband who is (in some way, to some extent) responsible for the death. I have arrived at this conclusion now. Could I – should I – have arrived there earlier? And if so, how much earlier?

Help me, Si, I can't do it alone. Nobody is that brave, that honest. In my letters – did anything ever lead you to suppose that in some sort of way I KNEW FROM THE VERY BEGINNING? Myself, I date it all from the moment I saw the face on the tombstone – some kind of awareness was born then, of that I'm sure. But then I think, *how* was it born? That day in Naples I saw Ferdinando with the child? Is it possible I saw him – them – walking towards me, not away from me? Was it Tonino I saw? Did I then recognise him on the cemetery photograph? Was that why I had that irresistible impulse to leave some kind of tribute on the headstone, however insignificant, however small?

Oh Si, please, please come for Easter. Come even earlier if you can. (And if you can, hurry to make your flight reservations – things get so booked up. Weather at pres is foul, but I'm sure it'll improve.) I know there are all sorts of decisions I've got to take, but when I'm alone with him I'm like a hare in the headlights: appalled, but kind of paralysed as well. Matilde is coming any day now, I will be trapped between the two of them, I need support, outside support. I carry on in zombie fashion, talking, smiling, doing all the usual things, but all the while my thoughts are tumbling around inside like washing in a spin drier, never slowing down enough for me to sort them out. And chief among them, in the foreground, a bloodstained sheet that is Tonino's ghost. I think I said that before, but it is the plain truth so I repeat it – style just now being my last consideration.

There are all sorts of questions that need answering too (or do they? Couldn't I just leave, just pack my bags and leave? Leave a note: I KNOW. He would know well enough what it is I know) – but the only one I can sort of make explicit when I'm with him, and even when I'm alone for that matter, is simply, WHO ARE YOU? These three words tap through my head like a drum beat, leaving no space for anything else. Who are you, Ferdinando d'Acquaviva? Who are you? Who are you? Who are you?

What a mess, what a godawful mess. Are you regretting the day you answered my first polite little letter? Bet you are. Oh Si, I'm sorry, so sorry to have dragged you into this, but please don't leave me now. You are the ONLY, ONLY person I can confide in. Lola.

From: salvia@libero.it
To: sparks@bookhound.com
Subject: to proof by common sense
Date: Wed, 12 Apr, 2000, 3.17 p.m.

Simon, for God's *sake*. I am in hell and hell is real and here on earth and I am burning in it. If, as you hinted over the phone, you think I'm going bonkers then the bonkers is (are?) real too. Hysterical? Of course I'm hysterical, that's the least I can be in the circumstances. And it's no good trotting out syllowhatsits at me. I know there's no logical validity or whatever you call it in my reasoning, but I know just as firmly that the connection is there. Heaps of perverts, you say, on Capri, from Tiberius onwards – why must it be Ferdinando, the one responsible for Tonino's death?

There's no must involved: it *is* Ferdinando. It *was* Ferdinando. (And I wish you'd belt up about Tiberius, this is no time for erudition.) I am not casting about for reasons to leave him, I have plenty of those as it is. Sometimes I fail to understand you: you urge me on, dismantle my defences, send me serious/joke poems that curdle my blood, rub my nose in shit like a puppy's, and now, when I've finally capitulated and opened up all the cupboards and brought out all the grim gory skeletons that were rattling about inside, you say I'm overdoing things, producing too darn

159

many skeletons. This one, OK; this nice old mouldy stinky one too, fine; but not that one.

May I remind you, Mr Rationality Itself, of a handy little instrument known as Occam's (Ockham's?) razor? Let me restate the argument you so object to:

– My marriage is in tatters and so am I; I come to Capri to recoup and write a book about (of all *strange unconnected* things on a surface reading) a paedophile. OK?

– My husband objects strongly and tries to dissuade me on both counts.

– I start – when, why, let's leave these aside for the moment – I start developing a parallel interest, *equally strange*, *equally unconnected* on a surface reading, in the story of a dead child whose photograph I (just happen to?) see in the cemetery.

– My interest generates (or so it appears to me) strange reactions in the local people.

– My husband, when he hears what I am up to, literally does his nut. Nearly throttles me, wrecks my computer, does everything he can to dissuade me from carrying out this third project, suggesting I go back to the second, which earlier he had tried almost every bit as hard to scuttle. Failing to convince me, he whisks me off to Tuscany, not because he wants me with him but in order to keep a watchful eye on me. Off and on he peeks (or probably does: I have no absolute proof because I wasn't keeping tight enough checks, but anyway he definitely does later, at least once) into my computer to see who I'm writing to and what about.

– I persist with my inquiry into the death of the child, and discover that in all likelihood the child in question was a victim of sexual abuse.

– By listening to my husband's voice mail and making certain deductions, I subsequently discover

Oh my God, Si, I've just thought: the voice mail. Remember that voice I told you I heard the first time I eavesdropped? The peasanty-sounding woman with a local accent, who asked for the *Dottore*, and I thought was probably someone looking for a job? Well, what if she wasn't? What if it was someone BLACKMAILING him? A member of Tonino's family, for example. Nico said he was sure they'd come into money, on account of the move to the mainland and the new business etc. I wouldn't listen to him at the time – it seemed such a *forzatura* (what's the word for this in English? Can't find one. Damn. Nmd. An exaggeration, anyway, a distortion) – but what if he was right?

Another piece of mosaic. OK, a putative piece of putative mosaic but it all adds up. I've *got* to leave him soon, I know. My mind is quite made up about this. The only thing I'm unresolved about is how and when, and whether there'll have to be a showdown between us or whether I can just sidle off with things half said. And if so – if there *is* a showdown, I mean – how I will react. Trombetta didn't say posh paedos were evil, exactly, she was too scientific for that, but she sort of implied it by the way she spoke: handling them, as it were, with a pair of verbal sugar tongs. Not too close or her fingers would get sticky. She had plenty of mercy for the yobs: virtually none at all for the poshies. And Ferdinando, like Fersen, is a super poshie. No wonder he identified with him, no wonder he resented my invasion of his territory. All these things strike me now

I'm getting all confused here, sorry – losing my compass. What I'm really trying to say is this: what happens if he collapses on me? Begs for forgiveness, understanding, help?

What do I do? Do I listen or don't I? Believe he's in good faith or don't I? I've loved him, Si, that's the trouble, perhaps still do. Can you take sugar tongs to a person you love, or isn't your instinct to grasp hold of them and stickiness be damned?

It's everyday life now that is so dreadful. I feel as if I'm walking on a goddamn tight-rope: one false step and I could plummet. He knows I know something – at least I think he does – but he doesn't know what, and he can't ask or he might reveal something he thinks I don't know, or hopes I don't know. These days are coldish but I catch him sweating – beads standing out all over his face. And then his eyes – they're on me all the time. We're like dogs: Mitzi's always frightened if another dog is frightened first – well, I'm the same, I'm catching his fear, and the other way round. Yesterday evening when I walked in with the shopping he was sitting in the sitting room in the dusk with all the blinds drawn, waiting for me like a spider, and I jumped so hard I dropped the bags with a crash, and then he leapt up, scraping the chair on the tiles, skreeeek, and we stood there staring at one another in this ghastly noise-filled silence that I couldn't somehow break because I'd lost all ways of communicating with him. The knot – the bond – it's there still, it still holds, but I can't rely on it any more, because I'm no longer sure it connects me to the same person. And it struck me too that this new person, this replicant, this Ferdinando look-alike, if such he is, might actually be a dangerous person to be close to. For example I

God, let me stop all this blather. I've read from the beginning and realise I haven't made my point at all. What I wanted to say with the bit about Occam's (Ockham's?) razor was this: Paedophile A + abused child + abused child found dead less than half a mile from paedophile A's home + all the other things I've mentioned = HEAVY HEAVY SUSPICIONS ON PAEDOPHILE A. You call *me* irrational, but to me it seems the height of irrationality to introduce paedophiles B, C, D, etc. into this equation – at any rate at this stage. The possibility is there, of course it is, possibilities sit thousands on a pin head; the likelihood, no.

Forgive me this long and muddled message. DON'T ANSWER IT or even be tempted to, I'll ring direct when I get a chance. Lucky I have Mitzi as she serves as a pretty good warning device, especially when we're outside on the terrace. Ears no longer perfect but nose still brilliant: she *smells* him coming, clever old dog. All I have to do is keep an eye on her tail and when I see the wagging . . . woosh and I'm out of the programme and the computer is snapped shut and stowed away.

No wagging yet, but still, better to be careful. It's not that I shirk anything, or am frightened in any way, it's just I'm not ready. Thank you, Si, for listening, and for being there, at the end of these wires or cables or chain of vibrations or whatever it is that links us. Fond love as always, L.

From: salvia@libero.it
To: sparks@bookhound.com
Subject: ed to torture
Date: Fri, Apr 14, 2000, 2.58 p.m.

You're a climber, you must have read that book about the one fellow who dangled off the end of the rope and the other who cut it and let him drop. Don't do that to me, Sparky, I beg of you. Not now. Later you can sit by and whistle and watch me fall all the way to blazes or Australia, but stay with me now, at least until I've done whatever it is I decide to do. I say this because I can feel you pulling away, and the mess I'm involved in is such, I can't say I blame you. Easter is out, eh? Thought so. Nmd.

Last night was awful. Last night he clung to me again. I can't sleep properly, haven't slept all night through for ages, but like this, with this alien, crab-like creature wound round me, half-supplicating, half-predatory, I couldn't even rest my body. All my muscles tensed up as if they were trying to create a casing, a layer of protection between him and me.

I know now what I'm afraid of because I've looked into myself: it's not his reaction, it's not his anger, it's not the possibility of violence (the business with the computer lead was pretty much a one-off, I swear, and he didn't wind it *that* tight anyway): no, I'm afraid of being drawn into his mind and having to fight his demons with him, side by side. I'm afraid of loyalty and its consequences; I'm afraid of being sucked into a bog.

That's what the defences are against: contagion. That was what my body was fighting against: involvement. And when he finally relaxed his hold and I finally jolted off somehow, through exhaustion, into sleep I dreamed Bosch goblin horrors that I don't even want to think about. Suffocating babies, small as stamps, wrapped in layers and layers of tissues, sweating, mewling, waiting for me with my fumbling hands to unwrap them and save them. A tiger, a beast, loose somewhere, but where? Pad, whiffle, growl, as it draws close. Me stuffing cardboard desperately against the window panes, hauling furniture to block it, and then wheeling round in panic only to discover

BASTA. My stomach burns all the time, I think I've got an ulcer or am getting one. You're right, I've got to break the impasse somehow. Facts? How can I come by them? You say start with the girl – find out if she's real or not; but it's no good my looking for someone I know nothing about except her Christian name. Elisa is fashionable in that age group – there was a whole spate of them in the eighties – should think the university is stuffed with them. Besides which, I don't want to go there, expose myself, start asking questions. News of what I'm up to might get back to F – Christ, he might *see* me there.

Except, no, perhaps it is quite a good idea after all, because if he did come to hear of it he'd think I was suffering from straightforward heterosexual jealousy, and this terrible murky cloud between us – all this unstated what-does-she-know business and does-she-know-what-I-fear-she-knows – would evaporate.

Temporarily. But it wouldn't last. Very soon we'd be back in square one again. Oh hell, hell, hell.

Anyway, like I said, even if this girl exists and even if I find her, she's probably no more than a screen and it's pointless talking to a screen.

The voice mail? No go – he's changed the code number. That in itself is a kind of proof, or no?

No, of course it isn't. You're so right, blast you: I've got no proof of anything, and that's the root of the bramble bush in which I'm entrapped. I've got no proof Tonino was abused, no proof he committed suicide, still less that he committed suicide *because* he was abused. It's all in my fucking imagination, or could be. Sterile womb: fertile imagination: bad combination: stupid hysterical bitch. I've got no proof my husband is a child abuser either, no proof he had anything whatsoever to do with Tonino's death, no proof – apart from a cloudy memory image stowed away for years in goodness knows what corner of my subconscious – that he ever even knew the child.

And yet I know these things with almost total certainty. If it were a jigsaw puzzle, say, or the mosaic I'm always on about, then it's practically completed in my mind save for one little piece. One little missing piece at the very centre. He's nervy, Si. He's rattled, verging on the seriously scared. When I look at him and he's not looking back my heart bleeds for him – sometimes. When his eyes meet mine I feel something more akin to anger.

Where do I find the missing piece? Where the hell else do I go and look for it? Everything hangs on this now: finding this one little bit that will enable me to act. When I find it –

if I find it – my problems won't be over, in fact in a certain way they will only be beginning, but at least the tension will. It won't matter then *what* I do – whether I stand my ground and have it out with Ferdinando, or run home to my mum, or simply run – at least I'll finally be doing something. And this poison I have inside – because that's exactly what this knowledge is: a poison – it won't matter in the end whether I sick it up or metabolise it, at least I'll be rid of the stuff.

Does this mean I'm coming round to the idea that I could, might, one day attempt to understand him? Maybe even forgive him? Better a millstone . . . I don't know, Si. I've been reading that textbook again, and it strikes me we're all of us such poor creatures. Does evil really exist? Or does it only exist where explanation breaks down and herd-instinct takes over? Better a millstone . . . Who can say? I didn't finish telling my dream: the postage-stamp child – when I unwrapped it, it didn't have Tonino's face, it had Ferdinando's.

Christ, what a shit pit. L.

PS Have just had a telephone call from Matilde, who is joining us in the shit pit shortly with her pug, relentless as a bulldozer despite all my efforts to deflect or at least delay the invasion, and have decided that *evil does exist* and she is it. Question: When is mine day? Answer: Never.

From: salvia@libero.it
To: sparks@bookhound.com
Subject: vitches and votes (or witches and wotes)
Date: Fri, Apr 14, 2000, 2.59 p.m.

---

dear Simon, how are things your neck of the woods? Haven't heard from you for quite a while. The Wcrft tome you sent is fine, but the other you listed doesn't sound quite my cup of tea somehow. 900pp is a bit over-newting the brew.

How are our finances? Have I any unsettled accounts with you? You sent a summary thing but I couldn't make out whether it was a reciept or a bill. Vitch was it, eh?

Maybe you've seen from the papers that we have regional elections coming up this weekend. Are you interested in hearing my opinion of Sig Berlusconi? If you are I will send you straight off, tit for threatened tat, 900pp of bilious invective.

Re Easter, I really meant it, you know, but I take your silence to mean in your delicate way you're not coming. Perhaps autumn then: during summer we live in a state of siege, and those who can leg it to Ladbroke Grove and places. Much love, Lola.

From: salvia@libero.it
To: sparks@bookhound.com
Subject: heading – provisional till I've thought one up
Date: Sun, Apr 16, 2000, 5.36 p.m.

He's gone to Naples to vote so I have hours. Oh what a *relief*, I can unburden.

Si, I've done something at last to break the deadlock. I don't know if it's going to be of any use or not, but I've done something, and maybe also found something, that MIGHT, just poiisib

From: salvia@libero.it
To: sparks@bookhound.com
Subject: is not a subject but an object in a gorse bush
Date: Tue, Apr 18, 2000, 3.52 a.m.

It's like a dreadful game of Grandmother's Footsteps. Look what I'm reduced to doing: creeping out of the bed in the middle of the night and blockading myself in the loo in order to write to you. (But maybe the real time won't crop up on your screen; maybe I'll have to mail this tomorrow; depends on my nerve and how deep he's sleeping when I come out. Anyway it's nearly three in the morning here – two with you.) On Sunday he came back to fetch his voting slip and nearly caught me in the act. Yesterday he shadowed me all day, today likewise.

He's everywhere. Physically, and mentally as well. Tonight he put on the pressure. Went all soft and pleading and tentacular – wanted to know what was wrong with me – wanted to talk about us, our marriage. Said he knew I was harbouring some grievance against him, but whatever it was I must bring it out into the open, and that if I did that he would do likewise. Because, yes, there were things about him that I didn't know – of course there were – all people have secrets and he was no exception. But a time comes in a marriage – rather like in a computer game – when you either overcome a great difficulty and move up on to another level together, or else you go on playing the same level with a different partner.

The comparison *froze* me, I could hardly believe he'd said it. I said quickly what did he know about computer games, and my voice must have gone funny because he stared at me and I saw – yes, it was fear, I saw fear in his eyes, Si, I swear. Panic almost, and in his whole body a kind of twitching animal alertness in presence of danger. He knows I know. I know he does, but he doesn't yet know that I know he knows I know. (God, how tortuous can you get.)

Anyway the moment was critical, I could sort of see him tottering, as if he was on the brink of a confession, but I was so frightened myself of what might come out, I couldn't give him the push he needed. Instead I forced myself to smile and say something banal about how hopeless he was with computers, and thank God the moment passed, and he relaxed and said something banal back about having seen someone play in the office, and we withdrew from the precipice, and that was that.

It's strange, but afterwards I felt almost close to him again, as if our shared wheelings on the rim of the abyss had demonstrated how dependent on one another we actually are. Standing together, falling together. Acrobats. Dance partners. Can't explain it really. What can be going on in my head? Do you think I'm gradually adapting, Si? Do you think that is what it is?

And if so, adapting to what? To the end of my marriage, or to being the wife of a paedophile, or what?

Or do you just continue to think I'm going bananas?

If you do, what follows will not reassure you. Or perhaps

it will. Because one thing I *cannot* do is to go on the way I am at present, and so I have TAKEN STEPS, in a very literal sense, to get out of this limbo. And in doing so I think I may have found something. But if I have, Si, or rather in order to establish whether I have or I haven't, I may have to ask for your help. And you may have to come here whether you like it or not.

The thing is this: on Saturday afternoon I took Mitzi for her walk, and we went, for the first time since all this horror started, to Villa Lysis. Villa Fersen. I haven't mentioned him much, but he's been in my head a lot recently, Jacques Fersen. Maybe the madness again, but I sometimes turn to him in my mind for enlightenment – ask him imaginary questions about what it was like to be a paedophile, and how a sensitive person like him could have got that way. When did it start? Why? Was his mother terrible, like the books say? Did she seduce him? Did someone else inflict sexual violence on him when he was a child? Did he feel crushed, humiliated? Was his story in fact not so different from that of one of Trombetta's yob paedos – a pathetic lifelong endeavour to recover lost dignity? Or was he – come on, Jacques, you can admit it now you're dead – was he an unrepentant dyed-in-the-wool poshie, all vanity and self-indulgence? (He doesn't answer my questions of course because he thinks I'm too crass and dull to bother with – just tilts back his aristocratic head and blows opium fumes at me through his cocaine-burnt nostrils. What do I, a Kensington-born housewife, know about his quest for the Sublime?)

I struck lucky. The caretaker was there, fiddling around in the garden, and when he saw me he recognised me and let me in, and said he wasn't closing up for another quarter of an hour and if I liked I could go into the villa itself and wander round.

A few months back I'd have been ecstatic – I think it was Proust said you could have everything, on condition that when you got it, it no longer brought you the happiness you thought it would. Still, it was interesting in a way. Atmosphere gone – totally: no whiffs of opium, no Alma Tadema nudes – all fresh cream paint and TV sockets. Master bathroom only place left intact. Wonderful sturdy hundred-year-old taps, a sunken green marble bath with seats inside, a carved shower-spout designed to pour fresh rainwater over the bathers from above – all such good stuff that it's practically indestructible. The rest of the house is the result of careful restoration work, but not so careful that it doesn't show. Opium den so fresh and aseptic it looked like a larder.

The only strange thing I noticed was that, in spite of the spicness and spanness and all the money that must have been spent on it, the place still feels abandoned, ruined. The views from the *salone* and the balcony outside are beautiful beyond description – sea, sky, Marina Grande on your left, Sorrento peninsula in front, and on your right the curtain of cliff below Villa Jovis, its folds all covered with broom and caper flowers, its hem plunging into the ring of peacock-blue water below – yet when you stand there you get the feeling (stupid to talk about places in this way, but I got it anyway) that nobody has ever yet enjoyed them. Or enjoyed the house or anything to do with it. An old jilted bride, that is what this villa reminds you of – like the old biddy in Dickens, remember, Miss Whoever she was, name began with an H. Waiting and wilting and going slowly to pot, then making another gigantic effort to tart herself up and start afresh with a new suitor, and then, when nothing comes of it, entering resignedly into another long period of waiting and decline.

But anyway, the villa's not the point. I left with the caretaker, and as he was locking up the gate I noticed a flight of stairs flanking the gateway – or rather two flights, on either side, one up, one down. I asked him where they led and he said they were public rights of way: the left-hand one went straight down to the bottom of the cliffs where there was a kind of bathing platform – you could hardly call it a beach; and the other was a back-way access to the Villa of Tiberius, Villa Jovis.

Short-cut home for me, therefore. I said was it safe, particularly for Mitzi who is not very good at slopes, and he said he hadn't climbed it since he was a boy, but he thought, yes, it was safe enough, provided you paid attention and stuck to the trodden path. The *cacciatori* used it sometimes, and their dogs seemed to manage all right. Had I taken Mitzi on the *passatiello*? I had? Well, it was much, much easier than the *passatiello*. Although there had been an accident, about a couple of years back, and it hadn't been a dog involved, either, it had been . . .

I said nothing, just let him talk. And this way I finally discovered the exact spot where it happened, Si. Not the mainland side of the promontory like I had imagined from what Nico said, but further along, right on the outmost edge, pretty well exactly halfway between the two villas, Fersen and Jovis. The caretaker knew because he'd watched the retrieval squad at work. He said they'd come up here with ropes and anchored them in place on the directions of their colleagues in a boat below, but nobody had dared lower themselves down them, and in the end they'd packed

177

it in, and rolled up their gear and sat down and smoked cigarettes instead. Lucky for them the body fell the distance it did, or they'd have had to have gone down whether they liked it or not – or someone would – couldn't just leave it there; but gravity had done its work, and in the end the boat squad was able to reach it from below with just a couple of firemen's ladders lashed together and a stretcher.

I learnt something else new as well. Although I think I would have figured it out for myself from the nature of the debris *en route*: this winding little track that links the two villas is not only used by the *cacciatori*, but also by clandestine couples in search of privacy. That set me thinking a bit.

I took the track, Si, and it is quite steep and quite difficult to follow, and at a certain point it sort of petered out, or else I took a wrong turn or something, and I found myself on steeper and steeper ground, almost scrabbling for a hand-hold among the furze and bushes. Mitzi was gone, and I was scared for a sec, but then I saw her standing in safety on what looked like a platform or an open balcony, several score feet above me to the left. So I clambered up to join her, taking a big detour round for safety's sake, and found myself on a kind of sandy ledge, carved into the mountain on one side and jutting out from it on the other, with some rough-hewn steps leading down to it from above. It was littered, but *littered*, thick as an Axminster practically, with condoms and used tissues and rubber gloves and empty tubes of lubricant and all the paraphernalia of alfresco sex. Not the sort of place to linger in, but I did – I couldn't drag myself away from it. I know you'll call it fantasy again and bash my logic, but I was convinced that somehow I'd stumbled across the very centre of the mystery I've been trying to solve. Here,

I was sure, was the pivotal point, the still core, the motion-less eye of the cyclone around which events had raged, and here, if only at particle level – in the quarks or whatnots – the imprint of these events was still perceptible. To anyone who had the equipment to capture it.

I looked up and saw against the skyline the outline of the little metal Madonna who stands above Tiberius's Leap and attracts all the lightning bolts – but her back has been turned for more than a century, and she could tell me nothing. Then, cautiously, shuffling my feet to the far edge amid the condom packets, I looked down into the giddy-making drop below – so high, so sheer you can't even see the rockface: only bushes sticking out from it, and glinty little patches of blue sea showing between the leaves. No wonder the *carabinieri* didn't fancy making the descent. And just as I was turning away, half drawn, half repelled, which is the way heights always affect me, I caught sight from the corner of my eye of something lodged in one of the bushes, something pale and solid-looking with rusty-coloured spots along its surface, that at first I thought was a bird – a nesting seagull or something – and am now convinced (don't groan, don't raise your eyes to the office ceiling: I'm perfectly aware it may be nothing sig-nificant) is a bundle of stuff – material – possibly clothes. I think I can see a string hanging down from it, but I can't swear. (A giantess's Tampax? Unlikely, *mon cher*.) Well out of reach, of course, and suicidal to try, but as soon as I get the chance – when Matilde comes, maybe, and F is busy fanning her with palm leaves and escorting her about in her electric litter and whatever – I'm going to come up here again with a pair of field glasses and see if I can make out what it is. If it looks interesting in any way I might try fishing for it, too, with a hook and some thread. And then if, IF, it does look interesting, and if, IF, I fail to retrieve it, I may call on you, Si, to help me out. With your climbing expertise it should be child's play.

Oh, I don't like that word, not in this context.

And now let me stop. It's rising fourish, and four is meant to be a moment of light sleep for all creatures. All, that is, save for your poor frantic friend, locked in the lavatory, gibbering gibberish into a machine, Lola.

From: salvia@libero.it
To: sparks@bookhound.com
Subject: haven't the heart to write a title, but you'll
          know it's me
Date: Thu, Apr 20, 2000, 3.29 p.m.

Passion week. Maundy Thursday. At the convent where I went to school this was marked out as the saddest day in the liturgical year.

Saddest day in my year, too. It is blood, Si, I'm afraid, or at least it looks like it through the field glasses. Dried blood, old blood. It's a shoe, a canvas shoe, a trainer, and it's COVERED IN RUST-COLOURED STAINS.

What does this mean? I'll tell you several things it *could* mean. It could mean, 1) someone had a picnic there and spilt tomato sauce over their shoes and threw them over the edge and walked home barefoot. That's possible. Or it could mean, 2) someone had a nosebleed or got their period or something, and did the same. Or else, 3) that some outdoor artist was painting a picture and squidged a tube of burnt sienna all over their sneakers. Or else, 4) one of the *cacciatori* shot himself in the foot, or hit a bird straight overhead that landed plop at his feet . . .

But I'll tell you what it means to me. It means someone had an accident there – a bad one. And since there's only been one bad accident there to my knowledge, it means (*to me*) that the shoe belonged to Tonino. And since it's bespattered with blood, and lies only about twenty feet from the place he fell (OK, from the place I *assume* he fell, but it's not as if there are that many others to choose from), it means he had another accident BEFORE the accident in which he fell . . .

I think he killed him, Simon, that's the short of it. I think he's not only a paedophile but a manslaughterer as well, that is what I think. Truly, soberly, reflectively. And I think I'm going mad, too, but not in the way you fear: harnessing my imagination to the steeds of hysteria and letting them whisk it up into the clouds like Elija in his chariot. No, I'm going mad because my head just cannot contain these suspicions, and nor can my heart. I am literally falling apart under the strain. All I could do when I got back was bury my face in Mitzi's fur and moan into it, no, no, no, no, no. Not this, not this cup – it is too bitter, I cannot drink it.

My own private passion – small maybe in comparison to many others, but painful beyond bearing.

So many little things come back to me. The money – my money – where does it go? Why does it go so fast? What does he buy with it? (Because, yes, I'm not sure if I told you, perhaps not, although the idea was yours to start with, but I've been riffling through his bank statements on the quiet, and there's a fixed monthly payment, made to a bank in Naples, which I can find no explanation for – always the same sum, three million lire, not huge, but not small either, and always the first of the month. I've found five instances of it in the papers he keeps here, two for this year, three for last, but if I had his Naples folder I bet I'd find more.) Silence, that is what he buys. Nico was right, he buys silence, and if it covers what I fear it does, I reckon it's quite cheap at the price.

Then there's the pity of the local people. Why do they pity me when, from an outsider's point of view, I am so fortunate? They pity me because I am his wife, and because I go around draped in my pathetic veil of ignorance, and nobody can rend it open for me. *Povera Duchessa d'Acquaviva* – you could sing it to the same tune as the ballad of the Contessa dei Carini – they probably do. And the clingings, the need, the nightmares that drive him against his inclination into my arms? His conscience, that is what drives him, his tangled, mangled, pulled around, distorted cat's cradle of a conscience.

I still don't entirely despise him, Si. And that's probably what's so painful about it all: I too am having to wrestle with my conscience. Only in the opposite way: holding it firm instead of getting it to warp. You'll have noticed, despite everything, I don't yet call him a murderer. If he killed – and I think he did kill – it must have been either an accident

No, no, STOP THAT, LOLA, it *can't* have been an accident, it *can't* have been, but it must have been in some way or to some extent involuntary. I don't know, maybe the child screamed or something, or threatened to tell on him. Or maybe, in the heat of the moment – desire – lust – an uncontrollable urge

Oh my God, I can't think of these things without my stomach heaving.

Wait while it passes. What I mean is, he must have lost his head. The person I know, the person I have lived with all these years, is just not capable of committing such an action in cold blood. Some mistake must have been involved, some blind moment must have come upon him, some wires in his brain must have got crossed.

He wanted me to have a child here to stay for the summer. A little Ukrainian child, was what he said. Don't they send them from Chernobyl any more? They used to. Skinny little blonds. *Adorabili*.

Oh Si, I can't take it. He has gone to the mainland to fetch Matilde. When he comes back – the very first moment we are alone together – I'm going to tell him I know. Everything. I can hold it in no longer. And then just see what happens. L.

From: salvia@libero.it
To: sparks@bookhound.com
Subject: me to no more scares
Date: Thu, Apr 20, 2000, 5.22 p.m.

Shrink time? Is that all you can come up with? Oh Simple Simon mine. Can't you see it's *way* past shrink time?

I don't see why you attribute such importance to those stupid elbow patches. I didn't say I *saw* them anyway. I can't have, because I didn't. At least I don't think I did: I saw the *jacket*, I recognised the *jacket*. I know his clothes, and I know that particular jacket has leather elbow patches sewn on to it to give a fake English country-gent look, and I mentioned it on this account – so you could see how it was I identified him so surely. And then, think: even if I did see them, it would only mean I saw *him* from the back, wouldn't it? There'd be no guarantee about the boy – Tonino. People who walk together don't always have their faces set in the same direction. Tonino may well have been looking the other way, or may have turned round to face me or something. Or maybe I caught his profile, or his reflection in a shop window. Anyway, the fact remains that I easily could have seen him then, and the elbow patches prove nothing, either one way or the other. I only wish they did, as this is far and away my worst fear: that I saw, and then, out of weakness or cowardice or God knows what, cancelled the sight from my memory slate. The other nightmares are nothing in comparison to this: that I may have been instrumental in a child's death.

And what in the name of blazes do you want with my mother's name and telephone number? If you want to help me, just be there, just listen. I understand your wanting to stay clear of this mess, but if you can't come in the flesh then BE THERE the way you have been so far, I entreat you, BE THERE. FOR ME, AND ME ALONE.

And for fuck's sake DON'T SEND ANY MORE FUCKING MESSAGES through the fucking e-mail. I'll write this again in the biggest script I can find, which is a miserable 36:

NO MORE MESSAGES

It was a miracle I picked this one up. I knew somehow you were going to, I could feel it, and so I stayed plugged in and caught it the moment it popped up on the screen. (Thanks for giving me your home number, though, it was really sweet of you, makes me feel a lot safer – bank holiday cropping up and all.)

Which is minutes ago, and any minute now they'll be here. Best be going. Two of them – how shall I stand it? L.

From: salvia@libero.it
To: sparks@bookhound.com
Subject: of the Moles
Date: Fri, Apr 21, 2000, 5.13 p.m.

They're out. Thank God. They've gone to the bookshop on Matilde's request. (Request? More like a decree.) She never reads anything except the deaths column in the papers: I think she wants to be alone with him – to talk about me.

The atmosphere in the house is as thick and heavy and sticky as Christmas cake. Cuttable with a knife. I can't help it, my anguish has turned physical and I literally fight for breath, for survival. I can smile – just – can stretch my mouth horizontal and bare my teeth at them – but small talk is pretty well beyond me.

I have huge talk to make, and it's lodged in my gullet, blocking all the rest. You say don't – you say go away, take time out, seek medical advice, calm it, calm it. I'm sure you're right, Si. I'm sure you're right too about the nervous breakdown – how the hell else can my nerves react except by splintering? But I can't leave, can't do anything until I deliver myself in some way of this huge bag of poison I carry round with me. I've got to dump it somewhere, puncture it, relieve myself of the weight. And in order to do so I've got to find out, like I said, WHO this totally unknown and unsuspected and unexplored FERDINANDO IS: whether the old Ferdinando that I loved is still there somewhere inside him, or whether he has vanished, overcome by the body snatcher and expelled, or whether there perhaps never was an old Ferdinando in the first place, save in my imagination. Once I have resolved this enigma and acted in consequence – I don't know, persuading him to give himself up, for example, should he happen to be the old Ferdinando, or wishing him to the devil, should he happen to be the new – then perhaps I will feel free to go.

I am waiting for him, spider-like as he waited for me the other evening, but he is elusive and/or commandeered. Last night he took my place at the card table, and restless though I was I never heard him come to bed. She must have nailed him to the chair. This morning he was up long before me, out buying breakfast tidbits for the cobra.

When I was a child there was a story that horrified me. Thumbelina, I think it was. The bit when she gets captured by the two moles, mother and son, and kept underground by them in the dark, and made to marry the son, and slave for them both, and never allowed to sing or dance or see the sun or the flowers or the fields.

That is me now: I feel I've been sequestered by these two alien beings who are using me, relentlessly, behind a veil of formal courtesy, for their own sinister ends.

The way Matilde looks at me – so piercingly, so measuring, so *aware*. Her intelligence is quick and grasping – she misses no tricks either at the card table or anywhere else – but it's limited by the fact that she can't hide it, can't feign ignorance, even when this would be the slyer option. I ought to be in the dark about the role she plays in her son's affairs – that would be the safest place to keep me – but instead I can see the old neurones ticking over inside her skull, under the immaculate peroxide hair-do (exactly half-way between grey and blonde, not an Angstrom unit out), and spot all the knowledge that is stored there. She is – not his confidante, I wouldn't say, I doubt it goes as far as that; nor do I think she either knows or wants to know anything definite about how he puts his tendencies into action – but these tendencies, tastes, proclivities or whatever, are not in the least bit foreign to her. Believe me, Si, she knows her boy.

And she knows something about my predicament too. Knows I'm not ambling along in contented ignorance the way I was before, knows I've stumbled on something, and knows some intervention is needed to right my course again. But what? What have I discovered? How has it affected me? Loyaltywise where do I stand? Am I a friend or a foe? Has my underground servitude turned me into a mole – one of them, one of their species, and as such to be counted on – or am I still an unpredictable little foreign being in their midst?

Oh yes, Matilde has problems all right, and she's out solving them now. In my dotty, detached way I shall be interested to see what she comes up with. My guess would be that she will probe first – gingerly, gingerly; make cautious little stabs and backjumps, as if I was a firework that had failed to go off. Never know, could be dangerous, could be just a dud.

I will feign duddery, I think. I want nothing to do with her: my account with her is closed. It is only with Ferdinando that I have unfinished business to settle, and that I must do directly, face to face, heart to empty heart.

Oh Si, if you have a God at your disposal, pray to him for me, will you? L.

From: salvia@libero.it
To: sparks@bookhound.com
Subject: still untackled but not for long now
Date: Sat, Apr 22, 2000, 6.17 p.m.

You are an angel. Archangel Simon. I *knew* you'd come in the end – it's that mountain training: I knew you wouldn't just sit by and leave me to my fate. This morning, I swear, after we'd spoken on the phone, I felt almost – well, not buoyant again but floatable, if you know what I mean. Theoretically. In the future. Like a noodle in a pot, I felt there is a possibility that one day – when all this is finished and only a dusty exhibit in my memory case – I may once again struggle to the surface.

It's given me the courage I so badly needed to have things out with Ferdinando. Because it's not quite true I haven't had the opportunity – I could have found one if I wanted, Matilde or no Matilde – but instead I've been snatching at any excuse to shirk. Too early, too late, too sleepy. Too cowardly. The thought that you will be here NEXT WEEK-END THAT EVER IS puts an end to all this nonsense. Tonight, or even earlier if the chance arises, I will banish all my heeby-jeebies and go for a showdown. I owe him – no, I don't owe him anything, but even the blackest criminal has a right to defend himself, no?

Then I'll get back to you with the report. You can see my spirits are slightly on the up again from the following little item for your collection that I think so far was missing: thank you, sweetest Simon, for being so **supportive**. Signed, LL. (One L for Lola and the other for Lazarus. He bobbed up again, didn't he, from a pretty low standpoint? Well, so will I.)

From: salvia@libero.it
To: sparks@bookhound.com
Subject: to a Complete and Marvellous Change of
          View
Date: Sun, Apr 23, 2000, 11.25 a.m.

Sparky, Sparky, Sparkler. FORGET EVERYTHING, THROW EVERYTHING AWAY – ALL THOSE REAMS OF BULLSHIT I WROTE, CHUCK 'EM IN THE BIN. Oh my GOD, have I been a twerp!

Tried to reach you on the phone to tell you the FANTASTIC news, but imagine you are cowering behind the receiver, wary of answering for fear of getting Loony Lola on the other end, and can't say I blame you one jot.

No time for proper explanations – I still don't want F to know about our correspondence, only the reasons now are a bit different. He's taken old Matty to mass – poor old Matty, how mean I have been about her, how paranoid and how unfair – and they'll only be an hour or so whereas I need AGES to straighten out the record for you.

In the meantime just this: that I have been mad and am now sane, deluded and am now informed, wrecked and am now saved, miserable and am now serene. Details following as soon as I get a chance, Lola.

*   *   *

PS One more (and I hope final) demand on your patience: could you hang fire over your visit here a bit, do you think? It's a question of tact, really. On my part, not yours. You'll understand when I tell you all. No, I swear I'm not hedging: I *long* to have you as my guest, if only to find a better thank-you present than the boring *baci*. Of which I would have to send a mountain to be quits, but now add merely a measly thousand or so of the non-chocolate variety, XXXXXXXXXXXX, L.

From: salvia@libero.it
To: sparks@bookhound.com
Subject: ive feeling (I know, Mr Fusspot, but I'm
          running out of ideas) of TOTAL BLISS
Date: Tue, Apr 25, 2000, 11.55 a.m.

The pug has eaten an entire Easter egg plus silver wrapper – brilliant animal – and has had to be shipped back to its own private vet in Naples. I have hours.

¡Olé! (¡Olè!? Which wé? Which wè?) Hardly know how or where to start, but anyway here goes.

Saturday evening. Imagine this scene: me in my madness sitting on the terrace in company of Matilde, pretending to read a book and wishing her a thousand miles away. I am all keyed up for the showdown with Ferdinando but he is nowhere to be seen. Instead there is this penetrating presence that has hovered round me all day: this wise, wily old face that never takes its gaze off me; these bronzed beringed old hands with their fingers tap tap tapping on the arm-rest of the deckchair; this voice, pouring and slurring its lazy Neapolitan lingo into my unwilling ears. She is driving me madder than I already am, and this is saying something.

Then begins this extraordinary conversation. Well, monologue really, because until a tiny light dawns in my

195

brain as to what she is on about, I am literally robbed of my capacity for speech.

She begins – unusually for her whose only topic normally is Matilde: Matilde *splendens*, Matilde *triumphans* – by remarking that she has noticed all is not well between Ferdinando and myself.

I stare at my pages. Turn one. Dip my head.

Poor Dodo, she says. He has got himself into such a muddle. But there – that's what comes of concealing things. Men are so foolish that way. No, not foolish: weak. It's weakness, you know, it's a dread of scenes. They're meant to be so strong, so courageous, and perhaps they are – in battles and places. Who knows? But one little scene, one little feminine stamp of the foot and a few sobs and a reach for a hanky, and they're quivering in their shoes. I discovered that with my husband long ago, before we were even married.

She chuckles and I stare at whatever is on my lap: I can't even see if it's a book any more, the contours have disappeared.

There follows a long silence, interspersed with knowing sighs and a few more chuckles, diminuendo. You've discovered his secret, haven't you, Lola? she says at last. I knew you would, sooner or later. Wives always do.

My diaphragm flicks up violently, the way it does when you're winded, but I still can't say a word. I feel as if I have been plunged, still awake, into a nightmare. Or into the crazy mirror world of Alice: the Red Queen. Off with her head! Happenings I can't keep up with, language I can barely follow. This woman's son is a paedophile, a dangerous one, and she knows it, and she is discussing the matter with me, his wife, as if passing on a knitting pattern.

196

I think maybe she extends her hand to touch me at this point. Does something anyway that makes me jump and causes the object on my lap to fall to the floor.

More silence and more sighs and tuttings that evidence concern. Oh Lola, she says, Lolita *cara*. Lolitina, Lolitina. Don't take it so hard, or I'll begin to think he was right all along when he said you hadn't the strength to take it.

My face, over which I have no control, must meanwhile be arranging itself into a questioning shape. Maybe my eyebrows go up or something. Hardly surprising under the circumstances.

I wanted to tell you, you see, she goes on. I wanted him to tell you. From the beginning. In fact I *urged* him to tell you, many times, but . . .

But? Again, it is my face that must have said it: my voice is still missing.

Well, in the early days of your marriage you were so happy, both of you. And then – the child business. If you'd had one of your own it would have been so much easier, or so Dodo thought. He waited for that. But . . . *ahimè*, you know how it is with secrets: they get heavier and heavier, the longer they are kept, and more and more difficult to tell. He kept meaning to, and I kept urging him to, but somehow the moment was never quite right.

Lola? Her face is suddenly where the book was: on the floor, peering up at me. Considering her age and a hip replacement she moves like a ruddy monkey. Are you going to condemn him for this? For putting your feelings first? For not wanting to wound you?

Wound me? I feel as if, between the two of them, they have drawn and quartered me already without a qualm. Why should a mere wound have detained them?

And he would have told you, you know. He would have faced up to it, found a way, I know he would. Sooner or later. But then came the operation. And you know how it affected you, Lola, that operation. You remember, no, how depressed you got, how miserable it made you? *Chianievi, chianievi* – you were crying all the time. How *could* he tell you, in those conditions?

First sentence I could really understand. How indeed? 'Ahem, dearest, you will never have children now, but not to worry: you see, I am fond of children, oh yes, indeed, but in a rather different way. Let me see if I can explain . . .'

Oh Si, I don't know how long it went on for, or when it was that that tiny little flicker suddenly sparked off in my brain, shedding at first a patch and then a ray and then a whole firmament of light. I don't know what it was she said – some weird-sounding nonsense about a maid they'd had ages ago, and Ferdinando being young at the time, and about it being her, Matilde's, fault, because you should never have pretty maids in the house together with young sons – fatal – look at Nino and the usherette – at least Ferdinando didn't marry his, bla, bla, bla. Although the school fees and whatnots and the monthly upkeep – they'd never failed her there. No, people could say all they liked against the Acquaviva family, but not that they'd acted incorrectly in this circumstance or abandoned the child or . . .

Oh Christmas daisies. Dawn at last. He has a *child*, that's what it is. That's what it's been all along. Ferdinando has a child, an illegitimate child. A son who lives in Naples with his mother, and who he visits from time to time.

Oh Simon, can you believe it? And can you believe my relief, my utter, utter rapture?

Oh yes, that you can believe all right. Although, do you know, it's funny, I think Ferdinando had a point there: if I hadn't learnt about it in this extraordinary way, I *might* have been knocked off course when he told me. Jealous. Sad even. Some other woman bearing his child – the child that ought to have been mine – ours. I mean, either it's the first thing you tell someone, before you even start going out together, sort of thing, or else, it's true, it becomes more and more important and more and more difficult to disclose, and more and more upsetting when you finally do disclose it. He'd painted himself into a corner as far as sincerity between us was concerned, and just didn't, didn't have the guts to wrench himself out of it. Poor Ferdinando. Silly, stupid, featherbrained Ferdinando.

Don't ask me what I felt like. Don't ask me how I reacted. I haven't a clue. Maybe I danced – maybe I snatched up Matilde and covered her with kisses I'd never given her before and danced her round the terrace, I wouldn't be surprised. Maybe I cried; maybe I turned to Mitzi instead and blubbed again into her fur. Or maybe I just sat there like a punch-drunk fighter, my head swaying as the news and implications filtered through.

What are those patterns, when you look at them one way and they're a vase, and then another way and they're two faces? Can't remember what they're called, but anyway it was like that: everything taking on a new shape, a new meaning. And all the while my heart getting lighter and lighter, and the demons fleeing like so many little black bats, and peace and happiness welling in in their place.

You were right about the elbow patches: I never saw the child's face, never saw Tonino. Thank God for that. Because it wasn't Tonino who was with him, it was the other child, his son. And the same for everything else: a different cause, a different explanation all along the line. The caginess about his past? Self-explanatory now. Our troubled sex-life ditto. The woman on the phone – the wheedly, local one: it was the mother. (Or the grandmother maybe: F says contacts nowadays are mostly with the grandmother, the mother being slightly bitter and difficult to deal with.) The monthly payments – they are for the child's upkeep: half for schooling, clothes etc., and half into a savings fund on the side. The toys are for birthdays. Oh, why didn't I ever think of it before? I would have spared myself such agony.

Of course Ferdinando didn't want me going around asking questions and making a fool of myself. The kid lives in Naples, but his existence is what Matilde calls a *segreto di Pulcinella*: i.e. everyone here on Capri knows. (Everyone, that is, except me. And on this head, I must admit, I am *not* so forgiving: I think it was dead wrong of F to expose me to ridicule in this way, but there you are, too late now.) And of course he didn't, and still doesn't, want me trumpeting the news abroad to people like yourself.

He doesn't even want me to tell my mum. Not yet at any rate, not over the phone. On the contrary, he wants me to make her think I'm still going through a very low patch, in order to lure her over, and then, when she's here, I can tell her direct. I agree with this, since it appears to be so important to him. Frankly I don't think she'll move a whisker – probably say why don't I adopt the child and have done with it – two birds with one stone? And maybe . . . who knows . . . one day . . .

The other thing – about having a child to stay during the holidays – was in fact a roundabout move in that direction. A way of introducing Giovanni – his name is Giovanni –

into the house without having to confess to me the truth about his parentage. Pathetic really, but you have to imagine the shame that is attached to an affair of this kind in this part of the world. Ferdinando finds it *inelegant* to have a son whose mother was a housemaid, that's what it is. He hates being the subject of gossip, and particularly this kind of gossip: salacious, faintly back-stairy, according to him.

Myself, I don't give a *ficus*. They used to train Roman soldiers, you know (of course you know, but I will tell you all the same), in double-weighted armour, so that on the day of battle they were bouncing around like shuttlecocks. Well, that's what I feel like: as if a huge weight has been taken off me, and I bounce, and bounce and bounce.

I love this man I'm married to with all his weirdities. I love Mitzi and Capri and the villa, and the walks we go for and the people we meet and the incredibly beautiful things we see – day after magical day, cannot imagine why I ever felt otherwise. Mould? Can't see it. Cats' pee? Can't smell it anywhere. And I love Naples too, and I love the winter and the summer, and the climate and the food, and I love Althea and my mum and dozens of other minor pals I've never mentioned, and I think I could learn to love Giovanni in time, and maybe fairly quick time at that, and I am even – wait for it – even coming round to experiencing something like fondness for the dread old eighty-one-year-old cobra.

Forgive my exuberance, skin-crawling to a sober boffiny guy like you, but I think in an electronic way I love you too, Si. I do, really and truly. L.

From: salvia@libero.it
To: sparks@bookhound.com
Subject: I discuss with you alone (and therefore not to
         be read aloud in the office!)
Date: Wed, Apr 26, 2000, 8.27 a.m.

A quick message, Si, to tell you the really best news yet. I wanted to write last night, I was so chuffed about it, but our letters – these proper ones – are the only secret I haven't so far revealed to F, and I didn't want to run the risk of him waking up and finding me at it. Not that it would have mattered, but after what had just happened between him and me it might have looked a tiny bit shabby.

It's down – the barrier is down. He made love to me, Si. We made love to one another. Put out the flags if you like, all the way down Ladbroke Grove: the more who know the merrier.

Why is an act like this – a physical, animal, common or garden conjunction of bodies in one particular spot, or two particular spots – so important? Do you know the answer to that one? I don't, but I just know it's as if I'd been touched by a magic wand. (And leave out the smut, Mister: wands and whatnots: it wasn't *like* that, it was poetic, it was momentous, it was earth-rocking, it was star-shedding.)

Do I know you well enough to go into details? I reckon I do, but I'll have to be quick, as he's only gone for cobra croissants and he'll be back any minute.

Well, it wasn't completely smooth-going – I suppose we've got a bit out of practice as a pair, as a duo – and I'm not sure either of us really climaxed, not in a technical sense, I know I didn't. But the intensity, Si, the emotion, I can't explain. Mind-boggling. Body-boggling. Drums in your blood, cymbals in your ears, the lot.

And afterwards he was so tender, so gentle, so funny. We got the dottiest giggles. I hadn't really told Matilde all the dreadful things that had been passing through my head, but to him I told everything. I had to somehow, it was catharsis, it was release, it was starting all over again together from scratch. I couldn't have kept it in and said nothing: I'd covered too much ground alone, I had to take him back over it with me and close the distance. The paedophilia, the Tonino connection, even the bloodstained trainer and the fact that I'd suspected him, my husband, my love, my everything, of murder – out it all came. And like stuff out of a hoover bag, the moment it was out it just crumbled away to dust. We laughed like kids – I nearly fell off the bed.

Later this morning, after he's finished my portrait, we're going fishing for the shoe, and if we manage to hook it we'll take the dratted thing to the police and let them deal with it. Like that, Ferdie says, I will convince myself it is ketchup and at last we will have some peace.

I reckon I have all the peace I need already, but I agree it's probably the best thing to do. Just in case by some strange combination my imaginings did have a foundation, and some violent act was indeed committed on that spot. A likelihood that my rational self tells me is extremely remote.

Regarding Tonino, well, the angst is over. I will always carry his picture around with me in my heart – somehow I can't erase from my memory those soulful, faintly reproachful eyes under their curtain of lashes and thatch of bald-patched hair: Lola, listen to me, Lola, don't leave me here alone – but I am resigned now to the fact that nobody will ever know what really happened, or how he died or why.

When I said this to Ferdie he laughed again, but this time more ruefully. No, Signorina Marple, he said, nobody will ever know, and to my lax Mediterranean way of thinking that's as it should be. Your English tradition – Bacon, scientific inquiry – all very admirable, but there are some things best left in darkness. Then he kissed me and said goodnight in a very special, rather touching, old-fashioned way – *Buona notte, moglie mia*. Solemn but nice – and took me in his arms and held me till I slept.

In the night I awoke and found tears on my hair: he was crying: fast asleep but crying his eyes out. What a complicated character he is. I love him dearly the way he is but it will take me till my dying day to really understand him.

Must stop now and prepare the tackle, ready for the Big Shoe-Fishing Adventure. May be rather tricky – F leaning out over the precipice with the line and me hanging on to his heels, or perhaps the other way round, seeing that I'm the lighter one. Wish you were here to help, then it'd be a picnic. How about coming in June when we've all shaken down a bit? Love as always, Lola.

From: salvia@libero.it
To: sparks@bookhound.com
Subject: journeys and travel
Date: Wed, Apr 26, 2000, 1.12 p.m.

Dear Simon, do I have any outstanding orders with you? I think not, but in case I do, could you please cancel them? Ferdinando is taking me on a long, long holiday to South America and I am shelving all my writing projects until we return. Sorry if this interferes with your planned visit to Capri, but the trip is important: should we like the country a lot, who knows, we may even decide to stay there.

Thanks for all your help over Fersen and Witches and Whatnots. If the change of scenery inspires me with new ideas, I may well get in touch with you again later on. Enjoy your summer and your climbing in Wales, and wish me luck in life as I do you. Love, Lola.

A NOTE ON THE AUTHOR

Amanda Prantera was born and brought up in East Anglia. She went to Italy for a brief holiday when she was twenty and has lived there ever since. She has written ten previous novels, the most recent of which is *Don Giovanna*.

A NOTE ON THE TYPE

The text of this book is set in Linotype Sabon, named after the type founder, Jacques Sabon. It was designed by Jan Tschichold and jointly developed by Linotype, Monotype and Stempel, in response to a need for a typeface to be available in identical form for mechanical hot metal composition and hand composition using foundry type.

Tschichold based his design for Sabon roman on a fount engraved by Garamond, and Sabon italic on a fount by Granjon. It was first used in 1966 and has proved an enduring modern classic.